No Cause for Concern

David Wishart

For Chris Longmuir, with a huge thank-you for her technical help and advice….

ISBN-13: 978-1477653777
ISBN-10: 1477653775

D1456472

DRAMATIS PERSONAE

(Only the names of the main characters are given)

Corvinus's household and friends

Agron: Corvinus's Illyrian friend, living in Ostia. His wife is Cass

Bathyllus: the major-domo

Lippillus, Decimus Flavonius: Commander of the Public Ponds Watch. His wife is **Marcina Paullina**

Meton: the chef

Perilla, Rufia: Corvinus's wife

Others

Alexander: Cleia's brother

Astrapton, Gaius: Eutacticus's accountant

Bellarius, Quintus: Titus Luscius's friend

Cleia: Sempronia's maid

Critias: Eutacticus's major-domo

Daistratus: an artist

Eutacticus, Publius Sempronius: an organised-crime boss

Luscius, Titus: Occusia's missing son

Lynchus: his slave

Occusia: Eutacticus's wife

Paetinius, Publius: Father and son. The elder Paetinius is Eutacticus's former partner

Satrius, aka Laughing George: Eutacticus's chief heavy

Sempronia: Eutacticus's daughter

Sestia Galla: Eutacticus's ex-wife, now the wife of Paetinius Senior

The story takes place in October AD38.

ONE

So that was that. We'd got Clarus and Marilla firmly hitched with only a few minor glitches, such as the senile octogenarian priest who'd overseen the ceremony deciding half way through the wedding supper that the assembled guests would really, *really* appreciate a song about an Ostian bargee, and now it was back to Rome and the same heady round of fun and excitement. I'd just spent a very pleasant couple of hours propping up the bar of Renatius's wineshop shooting the breeze with the punters over a jug of Spoletan and was heading along Iugarius towards a shave-and-haircut in Market Square when the heavies came up on me from behind.

You know that feeling when you seem to be in two times and two places at once. Add to it a moment of extreme agony as you find yourself suddenly sandwiched between a pair of overmuscled gorillas with biceps straight off a marble statue and you more or less have the picture. It was like being hugged by an alleyway.

I glanced left and right. And up.

'Oh, shit,' I said. 'You're Eutacticus's boys, right?'

The gorilla squeezing me on the left gave me a grin; I'd only ever known him as Laughing George, but no doubt his white-haired old mother had another name for him, probably 'You Bastard!'.

'Well remembered, Corvinus,' he said. 'Got it in one. The boss wants to see you.'

Again? Oh, joy in the morning; don't four years just flash past when you're having fun. And another chat with Sempronius Eutacticus, organised crime's equivalent of a crocodile with attitude, wouldn't even figure in a masochist's definition of the phrase.

'Care to tell me what about?' My shoulders felt like they had parted company with my arms and moved up to the level of my ears. My rib-cage wasn't too happy about things, either.

'No.'

Ah, well, short and concise. Par for the course, where Laughing George was concerned, and I wasn't going to argue. I wasn't going to try running or screaming kidnap, either, because if I'd learned anything from my previous encounter with Eutacticus it was to go with the flow, because if you didn't the flow was liable to wash you down a very deep hole and put the lid on.

'So we're going to the Pincian,' I said.

'Yeah.'

'No transport this time?'

'It's a nice afternoon. We thought we'd walk.' The grin

broadened, showing teeth like the cheapest bricks in a third-rate tenement. 'Besides, the boss told us you don't like litters.'

'Right. Right.'

Well, he was thorough, Eutacticus, I'd give him that. Still, I'd've liked to've been asked.

* * *

It wasn't a chatty journey: Laughing George wasn't to be drawn, and his pal had all the conversational pazazz of a brick. We headed in close-knit silence up Broad Street past the Saepta and Agrippa Field into the rarefied atmosphere of the Pincian Hill, where money - mostly new money - doesn't just talk, it struts its stuff with a megaphone. I remembered Eutacticus's place as soon as I saw it: tritons on the gateposts, score high for flash and zilch for taste, the worst the Pincian could throw at you and then some more on top. The statues flanking the driveway that led up to the house alone would've kept the quarry-owners in Luna in sturgeon and bears' paws for a year, and the greenery providing the backdrop had been topiaried to within an inch of its life.

Laughing George nodded to the guy on the gate, and we were in. Then it was past another half dozen of scowling prime-rate bought help, up the cedar staircase and the deferential tap on the ivory-inlaid study door.

'Come in.'

We did. The lad himself was on the reading couch, doing his crocodile-in-the-swamp-waiting-for-lunch impression. That wasn't the surprise. The surprise was the woman sitting on a chair next to him: a little, mousey, middle-aged Roman matron like a straight-backed dumpling wearing a hairdo and jewellery and just radiating Respectability and Traditional Family Values. If old Marcus Cato, bless his puritanical socks, had had a mum, then this lady was a dead ringer for her.

'Valerius Corvinus. Good of you to come.' The crocodile jaws spread in a smile as genuine as a tin denarius. 'How nice to see you again.'

'Yeah, well -'

'Thank you, Satrius. That's all.' Laughing George exited. 'Corvinus, this is my wife Occusia. She'll be the one talking to you.' He got up. 'I thought, though, that I should be here when you arrived. Just so we're absolutely clear where we stand.'

'Namely?' I massaged my shoulders.

'I need a favour, and in the light of our last encounter I believe you're the right man to ask. Do what Occusia asks, and I'll be very grateful. Very grateful indeed. Turn her down, or fudge things, and – watch my lips here, please – you'll wish that you'd never been born.' The smile broadened. 'Your choice, absolutely no pressure. You understand?'

'Ah –'

'Good. I'm glad. Now if you'll excuse me I have work to do.'

Scams to run, magistrates to square, bodies to hide. Busy, busy, busy. 'Yeah,' I said. 'Sure. Have a nice day.' He left, closing the door behind him.

*   *   *

Shit.

We stared at each other, the Respectable Dumpling and me, for a good half minute. Then she cleared her throat. 'He's a lovely man, really,' she said. 'When you get to know him. Pour yourself a cup of wine, Valerius Corvinus, and sit down.'

There was a tray with a silver wine jug and cups on the table in the corner. I went over and poured myself a badly-needed whopper.

'You mean he didn't mean it?' I said.

'Oh, yes. Publius always says what he means. But there's no real malice in him, that's just his way.'

Oh, whoopee. I took a major swig of the wine – first-grade Falernian, as if I'd expected anything less –, gave myself a top-up and took the cup over to the reading couch. Well, if my balls were properly in the mangle here – which they undoubtedly were – I might as well grin and accept the situation. For the time being, anyway.

'Fine,' I said. 'So what's this favour?'

'I want you to find my son. Titus.'

Oh, really? 'Gods, lady, if Eutacticus wanted me to find his son for him then why not just –?'

'No. Titus isn't Publius's, he's mine. From a previous marriage. Publius is his stepfather.'

'Same difference. Why couldn't he have told me himself?'

'It's complicated. He can't be involved.' She fixed me with anxious, mousey eyes.

'Okay.' I set the cup down on the small table next to the couch. 'So maybe it'll save us a bit of time if you just start at the beginning and talk me through it.'

The mousey eyes blinked. 'Publius and I were married two years ago. He'd been divorced for twenty years, I'd been widowed for ten. He had a daughter - that's Sempronia - and I had a son, Titus. He's just turned twenty-two. Such a lovely boy, and we were so grateful to Publius for taking us in. However, to tell you the truth, they've never really got on. And recently it's got worse.

Much worse.'

Uh-huh. I was beginning to see the light here, and it wasn't too difficult to guess what was coming next. 'Your son's done a runner?' I said.

She nodded. 'He left a note for Publius saying he was leaving, and if he found out that Publius was using his contacts to track him down he'd never see him again. He meant it, too. Titus can be quite stubborn, and he's just as strong-willed in his own way as Publius is. Publius was very upset. He was planning to adopt him formally in spite of' – she hesitated – 'well, Titus wasn't very keen to take his name, what with one thing and another. He never has been.'

Right. So what we'd got here was the old story of the domineering father – stepfather, in this case – straight-arming his son to do something he didn't want to do, and the son taking the simplest way out. I could understand that: I'd been through it myself when I was a lot younger than this Titus. And I'd bet that when it came to straight-arming, Eutacticus wouldn't exactly be subtlety personified. Still, the young guy sounded like he was no soft touch, either, and reading between the lines I'd guess that 'they've never really got on' was a whopping understatement. Life in the Eutacticus household over the past couple of years must've been fun, fun, fun.

'You have any idea where he might've gone?' I said.

'Oh, yes. I'm fairly certain about that. His...my late husband was an actor.' She blushed: in the social scheme of things, actors rank about as high as fluteplayers and jugglers, which means barely into the sentient bracket. 'An actor-manager, actually. He had a company that worked the north as far as Perusia, playing the local theatres. He took Titus with him as soon as he was old enough, and Titus loved it. Then when Marcus - that was my husband, Marcus Luscius - died his brother Sextus took over the troupe, and Titus went along with him every year, acting the female leads. Only when we married, Publius thought it wasn't very...you know, not the proper thing, and he stopped him doing it. Titus wasn't happy about that at all.'

'So you think he's gone off to join his uncle?'

'I'm almost sure of it. I don't know exactly where they'll be at present – it's quite late in the season now, so they'll probably be working their way back – but you could ask Sextus's wife Tullia. She should know.'

'She's here in Rome?'

'Yes, on the Aventine. I've written down directions so you can find her.' She took a rolled-up piece of paper from her mantle and handed it to me. 'Valerius Corvinus, I know this is... Publius goes at things like a bull at a gate, it's a great deal to ask, particularly as it's really so trivial, but I honestly am grateful.'

Yeah, right. Mind you, I knew how young Titus Luscius – presumably that was still the kid's name, if he hadn't been formally adopted yet – felt; it would've taken real guts to go against a stepfather like Eutacticus. And the chances were several thousand to one that there was no real cause for concern: he had simply – sensibly – taken off for the tall timber and was doing something he enjoyed for a change. On the other hand, Eutacticus had made it very clear that a refusal on my part to look for him wasn't an option, and messing with that bastard wasn't a hassle I needed. Trivial or not, no cause for concern or not, I was stuck with the job.

'That's okay, lady,' I said. 'It's not your fault. I'll do what I can.' I swallowed the last of my wine and stood up. 'Was there anything else? I mean, did he take anything with him? Money, for example?'

'I don't know, but probably. Money wouldn't've been a problem. Publius lets him have as much as he likes, when he likes. He's very generous, to both of us.'

Occusia stood up too. 'Oh, he did take his personal slave

9

with him. Lynchus. That was no surprise. They've been together since they were children, and they're more friends than slave and master.'

'Right. Well, it's a start, anyway. Fair enough, I'll let you know how I get on.' I was on my way to the door, but then I stopped. 'One thing. If I do find him, what do you want me to do?'

'Persuade him to come back. If you can.'

'And if he won't come?'

The mousey eyes blinked at me again. 'I don't know.'

Great. There's nothing like firm instructions from a client. But we'd cross that bridge when we came to it.

* * *

Laughing George – I supposed I'd better call him Satrius, now we'd been formally introduced – wasn't in evidence: probably he'd had a hard day's mugging and needed to curl up with a good book and a cup of warm milk. I was heading for the stairs, but I'd only got half way when a door further along the gallery opened and a girl came towards me. Forget mousey dumpling, this one was a stunner: early twenties, smallish but compact, midnight-dark hair and the poise of an Imperial. Sempronia, presumably, but if so then she didn't take after her father. I stopped.

'Valerius Corvinus?'

'Yeah.'

'I'm Sempronia. I was wondering if I could have a word with you before you go.'

'Sure.'

'Not here, please. In private. Come into my room.'

'Ah –'

'Oh, it's all right. My maid's there already.'

'Fine, then.' I followed her into the room she'd come out of. Not a bedroom, a day-room with couches. The maid, a wispy little thing about the same age, was sitting on a stool in the far corner, hands clasped in her lap and eyes lowered. Puffy face: she looked like she'd been crying a lot recently. She didn't look up as we came in, and the girl ignored her.

'Have a seat, please.'

I sat down on one of the couches and she lay down opposite me.

'You've talked to my stepmother. And my father.'

'Yeah, well, not so much to the latter,' I said. 'It was mostly one way. Let's just say we communicated.'

'Yes.' Voice as expressionless as her face. 'He can be a bit like that. Or a lot like that, really. I'm sorry.'

'That's okay. I wasn't expecting anything different.'

'I thought someone had better tell you a bit more about Titus. And the situation here. More than my stepmother probably did, at any rate. If you're going to look for him then you need to know the whole picture.'

'Fair enough,' I said cautiously. 'Go ahead.'

'Occusia told you about the quarrel?'

'Not as such, no. But there'd have to have been one, so I sort of took it as read.'

'Mm.' She rested her chin on her hand. 'It happened the evening before he left, but it'd been building for months. Years, really, ever since Father married again. He wanted Titus to be part of the firm. That's what he calls it, by the way.' Her voice was still neutral. 'I did have a brother once, a real one, but he died of a fever a year before the wedding. Titus was the replacement.'

'Only he doesn't want to be?'

'No. Titus hates everything about my father. He would've stopped Occusia marrying him at all if he could, but she talked him round. It was that or starve, or go crawling to Tullia and her husband. Did Occusia mention Tullia?'

'Her sister-in-law. Yeah.'

'Well, they've never got on, and she and Sextus Luscius are living on the breadline in any case. So Father it was. Not that it was much of a hardship. As long as he gets his way, Father's a pussycat.'

Oh, really? 'And if he doesn't?'

Her eyes rested on me for a moment, then shifted aside: okay, it had been a pretty stupid question at that. 'Titus fought a running battle with my father for two years,' she said. 'He wouldn't be adopted, he wouldn't get involved with the firm. Oh, he never got into an argument. At a certain point he just said "No", very politely, and Father didn't press him any further. That was the situation until three days ago.'

'The day of the quarrel?'

She nodded. 'Father took him into the study and told him he'd had enough. He was going to make a formal application for adoption, and unless Titus gave him his full co-operation he was out completely. He also hinted that he'd start divorce proceedings against my stepmother.'

Shit! 'He'd do that?'

'Oh, yes.'

'Couldn't he just have adopted someone else? I mean, brought them into the family as an heir? It's done all the time, and with his money he could pick and choose.'

'You obviously don't know my father as well as I thought you did, Valerius Corvinus. He'd decided on Titus, so

Titus it would be. If anything, the fact that Titus was fighting him every step of the way only made him more determined.'

Well, I'd believe that. Eutacticus wasn't the kind of bastard who'd take 'no' for an answer. 'Did Occusia know? About the terms, I mean?'

She was quiet for a long time. Then she said: 'Father told Titus in private, so it would depend if he'd passed it on. I don't think he did, but I'm not absolutely sure. And of course Father could've told her himself. A bit of moral blackmail. He's not above using any lever he can lay his hands on.'

Said without the barest smidgeon of expression. There ain't nothing like being popular with your family, and I reckoned that, daughter or not, young Sempronia's opinion of Eutacticus wasn't a lot higher than her stepbrother's. She was smart, too. 'So if it was private between Titus and your father then how do you come to know?'

'Ah.' She ducked her head. 'That's another piece of the picture you have to have. Another reason why Titus doesn't want Father to adopt him is that it'd make us legally brother and sister.'

'Yeah, well, naturally, but -'

'That would mean we couldn't marry.'

I stared at her. Oh, bugger; this thing was getting more complicated by the minute. 'You likely to?'

'Of course. We liked each other from the start, and it's sort of developed from there. It wouldn't've been easy swinging it even so, but as long as Titus was legally another man's son there was a reasonable chance. If the adoption had gone through there would've been no chance at all.'

'Did your father know about this?'

'What do you think? No-one knew, apart from us, because we couldn't trust anyone.'

'Then why tell me?'

'Because when you find him you can tell him that I'm ready to go ahead with a marriage now, as soon as he can arrange it. I'll meet him anywhere he likes.'

'Isn't that, uh, a bit drastic?'

'Yes. But you see I've no choice either. Titus wasn't the only one being pressured. Father's engaged me to a certain Lucius Statius Liber. Not a great catch in society terms, but his family's big in Beneventum and it's as high up the social ladder as someone with our side's background and commercial interests can expect to get. The wedding's in six months' time, after the Spring

Festival.'

Right. Right. Mind you, for all the young lady's manner of cool determination – and Sempronia was no fluffy kitten, I could see that – I reckoned there was more than a bit of astigmatism here. The boyfriend's choice of lifestyle might suit him and not be all that different from what he'd been used to before his mother married Eutacticus, but if she couldn't somehow bring her father round to the idea then unless she had a private income of her own sweet Sempronia would have to make some pretty radical changes to her expectations. Still, that was no affair of mine, and to tell the truth my sympathies were with the kids.

'So why didn't he tell you where he was going before he went?' I said. 'Or even that he was going at all? Or did he?'

She frowned. 'No, he didn't. Not a word, not even a hint. That's been worrying me. It isn't like him just to take off, however angry he was with Father.'

Ah, well, there was probably a simple-enough explanation, and I didn't know the exact circumstances. Maybe the guy had had to take his chance of escape when it was offered and hadn't had the opportunity, or maybe he was waiting until he'd made definite arrangements and would get a message to her.

Everything seemed pretty cut and dried, anyway. I stood up.

'Right, then,' I said. 'I'll see what I can do.'

'You'll give him my message? When you see him?'

'Yeah. But that's it, lady. No arm-twisting, not on my part. I don't play Cupid, and I don't play piggy-in-the-middle, either. Certainly not where your father's concerned. That suit you?'

'Yes. You won't have to. I promise.'

'Fine.' I glanced over at the maid in the corner. She hadn't moved, hadn't even, from the look of her, so much as raised her eyes from the floor right through the conversation. 'I'll be in touch.'

'Thank you, Valerius Corvinus. And I'm sorry about my father forcing you into this. It's just the way he does things.'

'Yeah. So I've noticed.'

I left.

TWO

'But why on earth did you agree to do it, Marcus?' Perilla
said.

'You've never met Eutacticus.' I poured myself a refill of
Setinian from the jug next to the couch: the first cupful
hadn't even touched the sides. 'You don't argue with
guys like that. It isn't healthy. Besides, it's no big deal. I'll
just go down to the Aventine tomorrow, have a word with
this Tullia and get details of her husband's itinerary from
her, then find the kid, talk to him and report back. Job
done. Occusia or whoever can take it from there and they
can all go to hell in a handcart as far as I'm concerned.
Like the woman said, it's the end of the season and
Luscius's troupe'll be well on their way back, so they
can't be far away. If I take the mare three or four days
should do it, max, and I can slum it in roadside inns for
that length of time no bother.'

'Hmm.' Perilla sniffed. 'I still don't like it. Besides, I've
arranged an appointment with Daistratus for the day after
tomorrow.'

'Who the hell is Daistratus?'

'You remember. The wall painter. About the dining room
mural.'

Oh, bugger. I did remember, at that: Daistratus was a

protégé of one of the lady's poetry pals who was touting him around (possibly for private reasons of her own) in the hopes of fixing the guy up with a few lucrative commissions. One of which was to fill the empty space on our dining-room wall. 'No problem,' I said. 'You're the artistic one in the family. You talk to him. I'd just stand around making polite noises anyway.'

'But Marcus! We have to agree on a subject, at least. That's a family decision.'

'As long as it's not dead animals or birds I'm easy.' I took another swallow of wine. 'What's he good at?'

'Rutilia said he specialises in architecture.'

'Fine.' A nice tasteful picture of a lakeside villa at evening, possibly with a boat in the foreground drifting gently across the placid water, would just do nicely.

'Architecture it is.'

'You're sure?'

'Absolutely certain. You've got a free hand. Surprise me.'

'He's...well, Rutilia says he's rather avant-garde. Years before his time, was how she put it.'

'That's okay. After all, how avant-garde can an architectural painter be? A villa is a villa is a villa. It's not like we're risking getting him to paint us a Bacchic orgy. Besides, your pal Rutilia wouldn't know avant-garde if it bit her in the bum.'

'All right. If you're really sure. But -'

'I told you. Absolutely certain. Subject closed.'

Bathyllus, our major-domo, drifted in. 'The chef says dinner is served, sir,' he said.

'Great.' I got up and hoisted the still-half-full wine jug.

* * *

I set off early next morning for the Aventine and Tullia's place. Occusia's directions were pretty straightforward, although I could see why she'd written them down for me in advance rather than told me there and then: having to admit face to face that her brother-in-law was an actor was bad enough, but she'd obviously felt that giving the contact address of his wife as a cookshop on the Aventine was something she couldn't bring herself to do. Yeah, well: marrying into money does have its downside, not least that it can bring a sudden dose of snobbery with it. I felt sorry for the kid, mind: the chances of a bit of maternal support for his decision not to fit in with his stepfather's plans would be slim at best. Maybe that was another reason why he'd cut and run without telling anyone.

The cookshop was in the same street as the Temple of Flora. There were two or three candidates on offer –

tenement dwellers tend to live out of cookshops, particularly when the weather gets too chancey for pavement barbecues, and the Aventine is prime tenement country – but I asked a friendly prostitute coming down the temple steps, and she pointed me to the right one. Sure enough, when I went in there was a middle-aged woman with her back to me chopping vegetables at the table beside the stove and feeding them into the stewpot. Another, much younger woman was decanting pickles into a smaller container on the counter. She looked up.

'We're not properly open yet, but I can do you some cold sliced sausage and salad,' she said.

'No, that's okay.' I glanced over at the woman with her back to me. 'I was looking for a lady called Tullia. Sextus Luscius's wife?'

The older woman turned round. I could see the resemblance between the two of them at once: obviously mother and daughter.

'That's me,' she said.

'Valerius Corvinus. I'm here from your sister-in-law Occusia. She's trying to trace her son Titus.'

'Yes?'

Not much interest there; mild hostility, if anything. I

remembered that Sempronia had said the two women didn't get on. 'He disappeared two or three days back. She thinks he might've gone to join your husband.'

'Really?'

'Mother!' The girl – she couldn't've been older than sixteen – set down the pickle jar.

The woman ignored her. 'We've nothing to do with Occusia any more,' she said. 'Not since she took up with that crook of a new husband of hers. Or with her fancy-dressed friends. You've had a wasted journey.'

She turned back to her chopping-board and reached for a carrot.

'Look, all I need to know is if he's been in touch with you,' I said. 'Failing that, where your husband's likely to be at the moment so I can check if he's gone there. It's no big deal.'

Tullia picked up the knife, then set it down. She didn't turn round.

'You look,' she said. 'I've nothing against Titus. He's a nice enough lad, it's not his fault he's saddled with that man as a stepfather, and by all accounts he isn't playing the same game as his mother. If he's run off to join Sextus then I don't blame him and good luck to him, he should've done it earlier. Now that's all I'm going to say.'

Bugger. Well, I'd tried. We'd just have to do it another way.

'Thanks for your help,' I said.

No answer: she'd gone back to chopping carrots.

I left.

I'd only got a few yards down the street when the girl caught me up.

'Valerius Corvinus?'

I stopped. 'Yeah?'

'I'm sorry about that.' She glanced back at the cookshop door. 'Mother can be...well, she can be a bit sharp at times. Particularly where Aunt Occusia's concerned.'

'Yeah, well. It's understandable, I suppose.'

'Titus hasn't been in touch. At least, not as far as I know. But if he's gone to join Father then he wouldn't need to ask us where he's likely to be. The troupe was Uncle Marcus's before he died and Dad took it over, and they've always followed the same route every season. Titus'd know that, he used to go with them until Sempronius Eutacticus put a stop to it. If I were you I'd try Sutrium. If they're not there yet they soon will be.'

Up the Cassian Road, about forty miles from Rome. Two days there, two back. Well, it could've been worse.

'Thanks,' I said.

'I hope you find him. If you do tell him Luscilla sends her love.' She was blushing.

'Yeah, I'll do that.'

But she was already gone, running back to the cookshop. Evidently a popular guy, young Titus, at least in some quarters.

* * *

So. I wasn't looking forward to four days in the saddle, not to mention the overnight accommodation in between: we didn't have any friends or acquaintances in that direction that I could scrounge a bed for the night from, which is the usual way of doing things if you very sensibly want to avoid roadside inns. Still, if it'd get Eutacticus off my back then I'd make the sacrifice gladly. Much too late to start today, though.

I went home.

THREE

Lysias the coachman had the mare saddled up and loaded down before dawn the next morning. I'd explained to our touchy chef Meton that I wouldn't be around to appreciate his dinners for the next four days at least, and he'd grudgingly provided me with a selection of goodies in case the substitute meals proved totally unfit for human consumption; which for Meton covers most of what's on offer at tables throughout the empire. Bathyllus supplied a travelling-flask of Setinian, and we were all fixed.

Getting across Rome on horseback is a bugger at any time, but just before dawn is your best bet, because most of the supply carts have trundled their way in and out and the streets are as empty as they're ever likely to get. Once I was clear of the city and onto the open road I settled the mare into a steady trot that wouldn't knacker either of us: I'm no horseman by choice, but the road was good and I could make it as far as the half-way point at Bacanae in plenty of time to suss out the possibilities for overnight accommodation. The weather was good, too, a cool autumn day perfect for riding, and the traffic when I branched off from the Flaminian Road onto the Cassian was light, mostly locals on foot or mule-back with the occasional farm cart or coach to provide variety.

I reached Bacanae half way through the afternoon. There was an inn just inside the town gates, so I left the mare tethered by the water trough outside and went in to size the place up. It looked promising: clean limewashed frontage, two storeys high, with stables to one side and a vine-trellised courtyard with wooden tables and stools on the other. The entrance was through the courtyard, and there were a couple of locals on one of the benches soaking up the afternoon sunshine. I gave them a nod in passing and got a suspicious stare and a couple of grunts in return. Yeah, well, we were in the country now. The inside looked promising too: lath and whitewashed plaster, a long communal table with benches running both sides like you'd see in any country farmhouse, beams with smoked hams and drying herbs hanging from them and a bar counter one end with an open door to the kitchen beyond from which a smell of stew was drifting. I looked up at the board with the wines written on it. Not a bad selection, with Graviscan and Statonian topping the list.

A guy carrying a pile of plates came through from the kitchen.

'Afternoon, sir,' he said. 'What can I get you?'

'Half a jug of the Graviscan would do for a start, pal,' I said. 'You serving food at present?'

'There's a game stew in the pot. Or the wife can make you an omelette if you like.'

'Stew would be great.'

He put his head round the open kitchen door and yelled, 'Secunda! One stew!', then turned back to me and set the plates down. 'You from Rome?'

'Yeah.'

'Nice place, they say.' He took a jug down from its peg and filled it from one of the flasks behind the counter. 'Need a room?'

'If you've got one free. A whole one, no sharing.'

'We can manage that.' He reached for a cup and filled it. 'Have your wine and food and my wife'll show you. Just for the one night, was it?'

'Yeah. At least, I think so.' I took a sip of the wine. Not bad; not bad at all. If the stew was as good and the room had a bug-free bed then here would do me nicely. 'I'm on my way to Sutrium.'

'Business or pleasure?'

'Business. I'm looking for a troupe of actors.'

'The Luscian bunch?'

'Yeah, that's the one.'

'You don't want Sutrium then. Theatre's closed for repairs.'

Bugger! 'Is that so, now?'

'They had a fire last month, took out the stage and most of the scenery. Or so I'm told. I haven't been that far myself.'

Hell. 'You any idea where I'd find them, then?'

'That's no problem at all, sir. We're the next stop on their route. Play's advertised for tomorrow afternoon.'

Oh, glory. If Luscius was due tomorrow then I'd timed things perfectly and saved myself a couple of painful days in the saddle. Thank you, Mercury, patron of travellers.

The landlord's wife appeared with a bowl of stew and a quarter-loaf and set them down at the end of the long table. I thanked her, topped up my winecup and took it and the jug over. The stew was excellent, and the bread was fresh out of the oven. Not too high a grit content from the millstone, either: with cookshop bread you need to watch where you're putting your teeth or you find yourself with fewer than you started with. Taken together with the not-bad wine, three ticked boxes out of four and counting. Mercury was definitely working his winged socks off; I reckoned I'd landed lucky here. 'You happen to know where they'll be staying?' I asked the landlord. 'The actors, I mean.'

'They camp out in the field next the theatre. You'll've seen that outside the gates on your way in. 'Less the weather's bad, when they use old Paquius's barn. But they'll be in the field this time for sure.'

'They come every year? The same troupe?'

'Aye, same ones. For the last twenty at least, to my certain knowledge. Same time, regular, just before the olive harvest.' He poured himself a cup of wine then came over and sat opposite me. 'Not always the same faces, mind, specially where the youngsters taking the female parts are concerned, but it's always been the Luscians. And you can be sure of a good show, so there's never any shortage of backers.'

That made sense. No one who's angling for a town officer's job would risk pissing off the voting punters by funding a dodgy production, particularly since - as it would - it'd represent a high spot in the local year. Entertainment opportunities in small towns like Bacanae may be thin on the ground, but where getting value for votes is concerned the locals tend to be pretty picky. Mind you, get yourself an established niche – as

Luscius's troupe seemed to've done – and you have it for life.

'You know them at all?' I asked.

'Can't say I do, not as such. They've been in here for a drink now and again, some of them, over the years. Just the evening of the play, though, because they move straight on. And they never make a night of it, either, because it means an early start in the morning.' He was beginning to give me curious looks. 'What's your interest, sir, if you don't mind me asking? Not in that line yourself, are you?'

'No, I'm just doing a favour for an acquaintance. The widow of the last guy to head the troupe.'

'Ah. Is that so, now. Carrying a message, then, would you be?'

That's another thing about these small towns: a stranger's an event in himself, to be milked for information and gossip. It isn't nosiness as such, just another way of passing the time and putting a little much-needed sparkle into an otherwise humdrum life. Still, I didn't mind, and I might even learn something.

'No,' I said. 'The lady thought her son might be with them. She asked me to check, that's all.'

The landlord chuckled. 'Run off, has he?' he said. 'Aye,

well, youngsters're like that. My eldest did the same, ran off to Arretium without a word said and signed up for a legionary. He's on the Rhine now and liable to stay there for the next twenty years if some bastard of a German doesn't hack his stupid head off first. You can't tell them at that age, can you? Still, if the lad's with his uncle he'll come to no harm.'

'You didn't hear of him, did you? Name's Titus.'

'No, sir, I'm sorry.' He drained his cup and got to his feet. 'Can't help you there, I'm afraid. Like I said, the troupe's only through here once a year, and if the boy's with them this time round you'll just have to see for yourself tomorrow. Now, if you've finished your stew I'll get the wife to show you a room and then if everything's agreeable maybe I could point you towards the town baths. You'll be wanting a bath badly if you've come all the way from Rome.'

I did, at that: sitting on the bench hadn't been a good idea, and I was stiffening up nicely. A leisurely steam in the bath-house, followed by a stroll round the town, another half jug of Graviscan and an early night would suit me fine.

We'd see what tomorrow would bring.

*　*　*

It brought a bloody rooster, for a start. The thing went off just before dawn, right under my window, seven times, and at full volume. Obviously a bird who scored high on job satisfaction and made sure everybody knew it. Ah, the joys of country life. Maybe I should ask my landlady what the chances were of a boiled chicken dinner.

The bath the day before had done its best, but moving quickly was still not an option. I gritted my teeth, gradually levered my pain-shattered and board-stiff body off the mattress, and stood up slowly. Then there were the hazards of the chamber pot that the management had thoughtfully provided and the struggle with tunic and sandals. Finally, I inched my way to the door, through it, and downstairs. Bugger. I'd still got the return journey to Rome to look forward to. If I ever got the chance I'd slit Eutacticus's throat with a rusty sawblade, and whistle while I did it.

There were half a dozen other punters round the kitchen table, tucking in to their hot porridge and – in one case – raw onion and bread. They gave me a nod and/or a grunt each as I crept to the end of the bench and sat down...

Or tried to. Bad idea. Bad, bad idea. I got up again with what in my present condition was alacrity. Hell. Yeah, well, I've never been much of a breakfast person anyway.

The punter with the onion sniggered.

'Porridge, sir?' The lady of the house, coming through from the kitchen with the pot in her hands. 'Or I could do you some eggs.'

So the rooster took the other part of his duties just as seriously. 'No, thanks,' I said. 'I'll pass.'

'Did you sleep well?'

'Yeah, fine.' I had, at that: the straw mattress had thankfully been free of bugs and fleas, I'd gone out like a light and woken – been woken – unbitten and without the frantic desire to scratch most of your skin off that tends to go with mornings in your average provincial-Italian inn. This place was definitely a find. 'I think I'll take an early walk. Freshen up a bit.'

'As you like, sir.'

I went outside. The sun was up, just, and it looked like being a fine mid-October day. The woodsmoke from the kitchen stove drifted across the courtyard, adding a tang to the earth-and-greenery smell carried by the breeze from the fields outside the town walls. Nice. I'm no countryman, but mornings in the country can have their good points, too. You wouldn't want to live there, mind.

I checked on the mare – she'd been comfortably housed, with plenty of clean straw and a full manger – and set off towards the centre of town. Not a long walk – you can see all that Bacanae has to offer inside a quarter of an hour and still have plenty of time to spare – but I needed to get my legs working again. I was planning on an easy morning: a shave at the barber's booth in the square, followed by a bath. Afterwards, another leisurely stroll back to the inn, some more of the Graviscan, or maybe I'd try the Statonian for a change, and a plate of cheese and olives, then over to the theatre to see if Luscius and company had arrived. A quiet day, in other words. Well, I may as well treat this as a holiday. Like the landlord had said, if young Titus had run off to join his uncle then he was safe enough, and no problem of mine. I'd be very surprised if the truth was anything different and the kid didn't send me away with a flea in my ear. Still, you had to go through the motions.

*   *   *

I got to the theatre just after noon. Obviously, the actors had arrived: I could see their wagon in the field next to it, and there were two or three leather tents pitched. The doors of the theatre were open, and I went inside. There was a rehearsal going on, or at least the guys were going through a few key passages and bits of business on the stage *sans* masks and costumes. I

34

slipped in as unobtrusively as I could and parked myself (painfully) at the end of one of the rows.

I knew what the play was, because it had been advertised on one of the walls in the market place: Maccius Plautus's 'Ghost'. Not the world's greatest comedy, but Old Flatfoot always goes down well with your average lowbrow audience just out for a good time, and I reckoned Sextus Luscius knew his Sutrians. The plot's simple: old father arrives home from abroad unexpectedly, interrupting his young son's romantic idyll with his no-better-than-she-should-be girlfriend. Desperate to keep him out of the house until the youngsters can tidy things up and the lady can make herself scarce, the smart-as-paint slave (there's always one of these) intercepts the old man and tells him he's got ghost problems: the house is haunted and has had to be shut up for the duration. Cue complications and a story line that's about as believable as a whistling rhino with feathers. Ah, the magic of theatre.

We were at the bit where the young hero's best pal reels in stewed to the gills and propped up by his own lady-friend. Occusia hadn't given me a description of her son, but the guy playing the male part of the duo looked a distinct possibility: right age, at least, early to mid twenties, and from what I could see of his face from this distance – I was right at the top of the house – there might even be a family resemblance. I sat up and took notice.

He'd got about half a minute into his scene when the older man standing in front of the stage watching things and making the occasional comment – Sextus Luscius himself, I assumed – waved his arms in a 'Stop, stop, stop!' gesture.

'Titus, you're supposed to be drunk, lad!' he shouted. 'Pissed out of your bloody skull! Come on, boy, let's have a bit of acting here! Start again!'

Titus, eh? Yeah, well, that was enough for me: we'd found our stray lamb right enough. I waited until the lad and his 'girlfriend' had gone through their scene to the boss's satisfaction, then stood up and came down the walkway.

I don't think anyone had noticed I was there up to then, certainly not Luscius, who'd had his back to me all the time. Now he turned round scowling.

'This is a private rehearsal,' he said. 'Come back in three hours with everyone else.'

I'd reached the VIP seats in the front row. I held up a placatory hand. 'Marcus Corvinus. And I'm sorry for interrupting. This won't take long, and it's no big deal. You're Sextus Luscius, right?'

'That's so.'

'And you're' – I looked up at the young guy on the stage – 'Titus Luscius?'

He nodded. He looked puzzled, and just a bit wary.

'I've come from Rome,' I said. 'Your mother sent me. She was anxious about you and she wanted to know where you were. She told me to tell you she wants you back.'

'But –' Sextus Luscius said.

'Also, there's a private message from someone else. She says she'll meet you any time, anywhere, to, ah, do what you were planning to do before you left. Okay?'

'"She"? What she?' The kid looked down at Luscius Senior. 'What's this about, Dad?'

Dad?

'This is ridiculous,' Luscius snapped at me. 'My wife knows perfectly well where we are, so her being anxious about Titus is nonsense. And what's this business about a private message?'

I was feeling seriously adrift here. 'Hang on,' I said to the kid. 'Ah...your name is Titus Luscius, right?'

'Right.'

'But you're not Occusia's son?'

'No. Of course I'm not. She's my aunt.'

Oh, bugger. Yeah, it made complete sense; there was no reason why both the Lucrii brothers shouldn't've named their respective kids Titus. Even so...

'Look,' I said to Luscius Senior, 'I'm sorry. I've obviously made a mistake. Your nephew Titus disappeared from home a few days ago, and his mother thought he might've gone to join you. You haven't seen him?'

'No. No, I haven't seen him.' He gestured round at the other four members of the group: two middle-aged men in the wings, the prepubescent kid on the stage playing the girlfriend, and the fluteplayer. They were all standing gawping at me, even the fluteplayer, who'd been well off to one side practising his arpeggios. 'What you see is what you get. You've had a wasted journey, pal.'

'So it would seem.' I gave young Titus another look.

'Well, I can only apologise again and ask you if he does turn up to pass on the message.'

'I'll do that.' Luscius didn't sound too friendly. 'Can't say he'd listen, though, and I'll tell you now I won't be twisting any arms. Titus is his father's son, and he's old enough to make up his own mind. If he's decided to get shot of that crooked bastard up on the Pincian then good luck to him. You tell Occusia that from me, right? Now. The show starts mid-afternoon. You'll hear the trumpet. Meanwhile if you don't mind I've got a rehearsal going.'

He turned away.

That was that, then. I went back to the inn.

FOUR

'He could still be our Titus,' I said.

Perilla shifted on her couch. 'Oh, really, dear!' she said. 'Isn't that needlessly complicating matters? Why should the boy lie to you? More to the point, why should his uncle? If he is his uncle, not his father after all. From what you told me Sextus Luscius made it quite clear where his sympathies lay, and that he was quite willing to shelter his nephew. He need only have said, "Yes, this is my nephew. He's a responsible adult and he's decided where he wants to be. Now go away."'

I sighed and topped up my winecup. 'Maybe they – he and the youngster – were the ones who wanted to complicate matters.'

'How do you mean?'

'Well, Luscius obviously has no time for Eutacticus, but he must know that the guy swings a lot of weight, one way and another. I know our Titus left a note saying his stepfather'd never see him again if he set his people out to look for him, but what's that worth? Particularly if his whereabouts aren't a secret any longer. What's to stop Eutacticus from using strongarm methods? Send his boys to lift him, take him back to Rome by force, then threaten to be very unpleasant to his uncle and mother if

40

the youngster doesn't co-operate?'

'He wouldn't do that! Surely!'

'Believe it, lady. Besides, he'd have nothing to lose, would he? So why should Luscius go through all that hassle? All he has to do is convince Eutacticus's messenger that he hasn't seen hide nor hair of young Titus and he's off the hook. Said messenger has to look somewhere else. And Titus isn't anywhere else, so the search can go on forever.'

'Surely it all depends whether there's actually another Titus Luscius who's Sextus's son.'

'Yeah. Of course it does. That's the only bit of light I've got here. If I go to Occusia – as I will tomorrow – and ask her if she has a nephew Titus the same age as her son, and she says no, then that's the game over and me out of things because my job's finished.'

'Wouldn't it all have been a little pointless then? I mean, as far as Titus and his uncle are concerned?'

I shrugged. 'They'd've had some time to think and plan, which is more than they had yesterday when I walked in on them out of nowhere. Apropos of which, if that young guy was our Titus then switching things round convincingly on the spot like he did was a pretty neat move. On Luscius's part as well.'

'They are actors, Marcus. Both of them.'

'Yeah. Still, if it was a performance then it was an impressive one, and totally off the cuff. Of course, they could've agreed on the father/son ploy as a failsafe, in case someone like me did turn up.' I took a swallow of wine. 'Anyway, leave it for now. We'll know for sure tomorrow. One way or another.'

At which point Bathyllus shimmered in. 'Dinner, sir. Madam.' He paused. 'Served in the dining-room.' The last bit was heavily stressed.

'Well, naturally, sunshine,' I said. 'Where else would it be?'

But I was talking to his retreating back. I looked at Perilla. 'What's wrong with Bathyllus?' I said.

'I can't think,' she said. 'I really don't know.' Interesting: those two gems had come out with a noticeable squeak embedded, and there were sudden spots of colour high on her cheekbones. The lady was lying. There was guilt there, too.

'Fair enough,' I said. I eased myself off the couch with what nonchalance I could muster — I'd had a bath as soon as I got back, but I was still pretty stiff and saddle-sore — and carried the winecup and jug through to the dining-room...

Jupitergodsbloodyalmighty!

'Ah... What do you think, Marcus?' Perilla said nervously. She'd cannoned into my back when I'd stopped at the dining-room door. 'Very...striking, isn't it? Of course, it's only sketched in at present. Daistratus said it'll take him another –'

'What the hell is it supposed to be?' I was goggling. Only sketched in or not, the full horror that would be the finished article was already pretty obvious.

'It's...well, it's...architectural. You said you wanted architecture.'

'Yeah, but I'd sort of expected an actual building to be involved somewhere.' Gods, the more you looked at it the worse it got. My brain had gone numb. 'Which way's up?'

'Don't be silly, dear, it's...' Perilla paused. 'Oh. I see what you mean. Those arches on the right. And the staircase joining the first and second floors.'

Bloody hell! I didn't even want to *look* at the staircase joining the first and second floors. I was having enough trouble with the normal three dimensions without bothering with a fourth. Or – I glanced at the arches, and my brain reeled afresh – a fifth and sixth. I wrenched my eyes away before the thing drew me in and swallowed me altogether.

43

'What does he call it?' I said.

'Er...*Fantasy Architecturescape Seven*,' Perilla said.

'You mean there are six more of these bastards somewhere?'

'Presumably. You said to surprise you.'

'Yeah. Right. And you've succeeded. Congratulations.'

Well, it explained Bathyllus's grump. If you sliced him into wafer-thin layers you'd find 'traditionalist' lettered all the way through. Life for the foreseeable future was going to be hell. 'I think a bucket of lime wash is in order. Or we can just ask this Daistratus to rub it out and give us something decent.'

'But we can't do that, dear! Everyone agrees that he's an artistic giant, a genius. And you have to admit that it is clever.'

'So's a fucking tightrope-walking elephant, but that doesn't mean I want one in my dining-room. Come on, Perilla! That thing's bad enough now. When it's finished, two or three days staring at it while we eat and our brains'll be mush!'

'Nonsense. It just takes a little getting used to.' She sniffed, but I noticed that she didn't look back at the picture. 'We can always do things gradually. Alter the seating arrangements. Move the dining couches so that they're sideways on. Marcus, it's a masterpiece! Besides, it wasn't cheap. And I paid in advance.'

I groaned.

Bathyllus came in. You could've used the little bald-head's expression to slice marble.

'Shall I bring the starters, sir?' he said.

'Yeah. Yeah, you do that. And, ah, move these couches round through ninety degrees, will you, pal? There's a bit of a draft from the door this evening.'

'Yes, sir. Certainly. Would you be wanting another jug of lime?'

'Pardon?'

'Wine, sir. I meant wine. I'm sorry. A slip of the tongue.'

'Right. Yes. Sure. Oh, and Bathyllus?'

'Yes, sir?'

'Make it the Special, will you?'

'The Special it is, sir.'

I reckoned if I was to get through this meal with my sanity intact I'd need all the anaesthetising I could get.

* * *

Next morning, I went back up to the Pincian to make my report. I'd scarcely given my cloak to the door-slave – the weather had turned colder – before Sempronia came out of the atrium and hurried towards me.

'Have you found him?' she said.

'That depends.' I followed her inside.

She frowned. 'Depends on what?'

Best get it over with. 'Does Sextus Luscius have a son?' I said.

The frown deepened. 'Yes. Yes he does. Why should you –?'

'His name Titus as well?'

'Yes, actually, it is. What does that have to do with anything?'

Bugger. 'And they're roughly the same age? The two Tituses, I mean.'

'Almost exactly.' We were in the atrium now, all bronze and marble statues, gilt couches and pricey murals. Flash, flash, flash. I sat down on one of the gilt couches, and she sat opposite me. 'There's only two months between them. Corvinus, what's this about? Did you see Titus or not?'

Well, we might as well be absolutely clear about this.

'Just a second, lady. Would this other Titus be about five eight, thinnish with dark curly hair?'

'I can't remember. I only saw him once, at the wedding, but he could be.'

'Okay. How about your one. Any distinguishing features?'

46

'Yes.' She was looking mystified. 'Quite a noticeable one, actually. He has a big chunk missing out of his right ear.' Her finger dabbed at her own ear; the lobe and a half-inch or so above. 'A dog bit him when he was five.'

Hell; that was that, then. Proof positive: the Titus Luscius I'd seen had definitely had both ears intact.

'Then the answer's no, I'm afraid. I didn't see him.'

'You're sure?' She looked lost. 'You're absolutely sure he wasn't there?'

'Absolutely.' I told her about my visit to the theatre and the conversation with Luscius.

'But he could've been... I don't know, inside one of the tents,' she said when I'd finished. 'Or behind the scenery somewhere. You didn't look?'

'No. But it isn't likely. He can't've known I was coming, so he'd have no reason to hide. If he'd been involved in the play – and he would've been, because he had acting experience – he'd've been out in the open with the rest, rehearsing. Those troupes don't carry passengers. Look, Sempronia, I'm sorry.'

She was quiet for a long time. Then she said: 'That's all right. At least it isn't, but it's not your fault. So if he isn't with his uncle then where is he?'

'I don't know.' I made up my mind. 'It's not the end of the

world. We'll just have to try something else, that's all. He didn't talk to you before he went?'

'No! I told you!'

'Gently, gently. Fine. Did he talk to anyone else?'

'No. Not that I know of. Astrapton saw him go, but I don't think –'

'Who's Astrapton?'

'Father's accountant. But he only saw him go through the gate, him and Lynchus.' Oh, yeah; the body-slave. Occusia had mentioned that Titus had taken him with him. 'I don't think they actually talked. They wouldn't. Titus ignored Astrapton, like he did all Father's business employees.'

'And Astrapton is where?'

'He has an office in the east wing.'

'Fine. Well, I'll talk to Astrapton before I leave. Just to check. Now. How about friends? People he might've confided in?'

'If he didn't tell me where he was going, Corvinus, then he'd be hardly likely to –'

'Yeah. Yeah, I know. But just in case. You got a name you can give me? Of a best friend?'

'You could try Quintus Bellarius. They go out drinking together.'

'And where would I find him?'

'I don't know. He's Titus's friend, not mine, and we've only met once or twice.'

'But –'

'Father doesn't like me getting too involved with Titus outside the house, especially since my engagement to Liber, so I don't really know any of his friends except by name. And of course we haven't wanted to do anything that would make Father suspicious. Ask at the Three Elms, they go there quite often. You'd've passed it on the way here, down Pincian Road between the Gardens of Pompey and Lucullus. They might be able to help.'

Yeah, and I remembered the place from the last time, four years back: pricey and pretentious as hell, but they'd had some of the best Velletrian I'd ever tasted. 'Right. I'll try that.'

'Do you think you'll find him? Titus, I mean.'

I gave her the honest answer. 'Maybe. I'll do my best, anyway. If we're lucky he may even be shacked up with that friend of his.' I stood up. 'I won't disturb your mother, particularly since it's bad news. You want to show me where this Astrapton hangs out?'

She got up too. 'Yes, of course. I'll get a slave to take you.' She raised her voice. 'Celer!'

One of the bought help materialised out of nowhere. Right; sign of an efficient household and top-rate bought help. You don't see them until you need them, and then they've been there all the time.

'Yes, miss,' the slave said.

'Take Valerius Corvinus to Astrapton's office.'

'Yes, miss. This way, sir.'

I went to talk to the accountant.

FIVE

'Office' was dignifying things: it was hardly bigger than a cubby-hole furnished with desk, chair, visitor's stool and wax-tablet-filled bookshelves. Astrapton was sitting on the second of the list. The guy was your typical sharp-as-they-come-and-going-places young Greek: thick, blue-black curly hair under his freedman's cap scented with oil I could smell from two yards away, limpid blue-black eyes, blue-black designer stubble, a snazzy Greek-style tunic and a selection of rings on his fingers that must've cost half of his yearly income.

'Good morning, sir,' he said when I walked in. 'What can I do for you?'

'Valerius Corvinus,' I said. 'Your boss's wife asked me to trace her missing son.'

He blinked. 'Oh, yes? Then I'm sorry, but I'm afraid I can't help you there.'

'You were the last one to see them, I understand.' I pulled up the stool and sat down in front of the desk. 'Him and his slave. Going out of the gate. That correct?'

'Ah…yes. Yes, it is.'

'Did you talk to them at all?'

'I didn't talk to Titus at any time. Or rather, he didn't talk to me.'

51

Yeah, well. Fair enough. Sempronia had already said that the guy didn't mix with his father's business underlings on principle. 'Okay. Just the details, then. Were they on foot?'

'Yes.'

'Carrying anything?'

'The slave had a couple of bags.'

'And you weren't suspicious?'

'Why should I be? Where they were going, if they were going anywhere, and what they were carrying was none of my business. And even if I had asked Luscius wouldn't't've told me.'

'Fine. And what time was this exactly?'

'Just before dawn.'

'*Before* dawn? That not a little early for you to be going out on business, pal? I assume it was business.'

'Yes, it was. But no, it wasn't unusual. The master wanted me to see someone urgently, and the person concerned wasn't free later in the day. That happens quite often in my job. The hours aren't what you'd call regular.'

Yeah, well: considering the nature of Eutacticus's business concerns perhaps it wasn't an avenue I wanted to explore. 'So you saw which direction they took? Titus and the slave?'

He looked fazed for a moment. 'Pardon?'

'If you followed them out the gate, pal, then you must've seen which way they went. Left or right? Away from the city centre or towards it?'

He frowned. 'Oh. Oh, yes. I see what you mean. But I can't help you there either. I didn't go out of the gate immediately. I realised I'd forgotten a document I needed, so I went back for it.'

'Pity.' Well, maybe the gate slave'd remember. I could ask him on my way out. 'So. You're absolutely sure about all this?' For what it was worth. Jupiter!

'Yes. Yes, I am.'

'Anything else you can tell me?'

'No.'

I shrugged and stood up. 'Fine. Thanks for your time.'

'You're very welcome,' he said, and went back to juggling the books.

I left. But I left puzzled. Eutacticus's tame books-juggler had been forthcoming enough, sure, if you could call giving me practically zilch in the way of information being forthcoming. All the same, there'd been something slightly wrong about that interview: there was the hesitation over the answers for a start, and I'd definitely seen a flash of relief on his face when he'd picked up the pen at the end of it. Astrapton had more beans to spill, I'd've bet a dozen of Eutacticus's Falernian on that. Trouble was, I was damned if I knew what they could be, and why he hadn't spilled them.

*　*　*

On my way out, I stopped by the muscle-bound gorilla who doubled as gate-keeper.

He gave me a suspicious look. 'Yeah?'

'No problem, pal,' I said. 'I was just hoping that you could cast your mind back to seven days ago. Just before dawn, the morning young Master Titus disappeared.'

'Yeah?'

'You were on the gate then?'

'Yeah.'

Well, I supposed that the fact that he could talk at all was a minor miracle in itself. And a vocabulary of one syllable is better than nothing.

'You saw them go out, right?'

'Could've done.'

Hey! A variation! 'Fine. Which direction did they –?'

'I said I could've done.'

Gods! 'Which is it, pal? Did you see them go or didn't you?'

'Could be either.'

Bugger; we were definitely verging on the philosophical here. 'You care to choose one, maybe?'

He stood up slowly. He topped me by a head and more than the corresponding width between the shoulders. 'Look, sir,' he said. 'Strangers coming in I notice, right? That is my job, because if they don't have no legit business they don't go no further. You ask me about strangers coming in, I'll tell you. I got a good memory for strangers coming in. Family going out, that's a different thing. The master, the mistress, the kids, they're in and out of here like a high priest in a brothel every fucking hour of every fucking day in the calendar. And when you're a gate slave one fucking day is the same as another. So the answer where your seven days ago is concerned is I could've done. You get me?'

I sighed. 'Yeah, I get you, pal. Could've done it is.'

'Fine.' He sat down again. 'So long as we're clear about it. Have a nice day, sir.'

Well, that was that. It would've been nice to have got a bit of corroboration, though, because when push came to shove I didn't trust Astrapton more than half. Then again, maybe I was imagining things and the guy just had the ordinary guilty conscience natural to all creative accountants.

Okay. Next stop the Three Elms to see if I could trace Titus's pal Quintus Bellarius. It was getting on for half way through the day in any case, and I reckoned I was due a half jug of wine. Or maybe just a cup, unless they'd lowered their prices since last time.

*   *   *

It wasn't far, just down the hill: a swanky place that you'd've taken for a private residence if it hadn't been for the dozen-odd tables on the lawn and the waiters going back and forth with trays of food and drinks. We hadn't quite hit the lunchtime spot yet, so apart from a couple of elderly narrow-stripers cornering the sylphium market between them I had the place to myself.

A waiter came over. 'Good morning, sir. What can I get you?'

'A cup of your best Velletrian would do fine, pal,' I said, pulling up a stool at the nearest table.

His delicately-trimmed eyebrows lifted. 'Just a cup?'

'As ever is.'

'Anything to eat?'

'No, no, I'm fine.'

'A cup of wine. Thank you, sir.' He sniffed and turned to go.

56

'Wait a minute,' I said. He turned back. 'You happen to know someone by the name of Quintus Bellarius?'

'Of course, sir. He's a regular customer.' With just the smidgeon of a stress on 'regular'.

'Know where I can find him?'

'His father's house is just down the hill. About two hundred yards, on the right.'

Well, that couldn't be handier. 'Thanks, pal.'

The Velletrian was as good as I remembered it. And as expensive. I took my time over it, then headed off towards the Bellarius place.

*   *   *

Quintus Bellarius was a little chubby guy who looked like he'd roll back up if you pushed him over. When the slave showed me through, he was sitting in a gazebo in the garden, holding a wax tablet and chewing on the blunt end of a stylus. His tunic was scruffier even than my own personal favourite that Perilla had unilaterally got rid of in one of her sporadic clothing purges, and its predominant colour was ink.

Not in the running for Snappily-Dressed Playboy of the Month, then.

'You don't happen to know a two-syllable synonym for "besotted", do you?' he said before I'd even spoken.

'Ah... "Stricken"?'

He beamed and made a note on the tablet. 'Yeah. "Stricken" is perfect. I like "stricken". You're a poet?'

'Uh, uh. Not me. That's my wife's department.'

'Your wife?'

'Rufia Perilla. I'm -'

He set the tablet down on the table beside him. 'Wow! Ovidius Naso's stepdaughter?'

'Yeah. That's her.'

The slave who'd brought me was still hovering.

'Callias, fetch us some wine, would you?' Bellarius said to him. 'And a stool for...?' He looked at me inquiringly.

'Corvinus. Valerius Corvinus.'

The slave left.

'You think you could give me an introduction?' Bellarius said. 'To your wife, I mean.' He was practically salivating.

I grinned. No ulterior motive there: the guy's interest was purely artistic, I was sure of that. Definitely not your standard sharp lad about town, this one. 'Sure,' I said. 'I could manage that.'

'Great! Now. What was it you wanted again?'

'I was hoping you might be able to tell me something about your friend Titus Luscius.'

'Titus? What about him?'

'You know he's disappeared?'

'How do you mean, "disappeared"?'

I shrugged. 'Just that. He left home seven days ago without telling anyone he was going, and he hasn't been back since. His mother's asked me to find him. You happen to know where he might be?'

He was staring at me. 'Not a clue.'

'When was the last time you saw him?'

'We had a jug of wine together at the Three Elms. That'd be, what, about ten or twelve days ago. You say he told nobody?'

'No one in the family, anyway.'

'That's not like Titus. He doesn't get on with his stepfather, sure, but his mother and stepsister are a different thing altogether.'

'He didn't even drop any hints to you? When you last saw him, I mean.'

'Uh-uh.'

'And he didn't seem, ah, worried about anything in particular? Or out of the ordinary in any way?'

'No, he was fine. We just chatted, like we always do.'

The slave came back with the stool and the wine tray. I sat down. The wine was Caecuban. *Good* Caecuban. I didn't know what Bellarius Senior did for a living, but he obviously wasn't short of a silver piece or two.

'Okay,' I said. 'Let's go over the possibilities. Where *could* he have gone? If, say, he'd had a bust-up with his stepfather and decided to leave home in a hurry.'

He shot me a look. 'That what happened?'

'Probably. The bust-up, certainly, the day before he left.'

'Over the adoption business?'

I nodded. 'He told you about that?'

'Oh, sure. That'd been going on for months. Years, even, practically since his mother's wedding. Titus wasn't having any of it. His stepfather's a crook. Not just someone who'll cut a corner to make a bit of extra profit, every businessman in Rome does that, my father included, but an actual crook. Titus has no time for him. He doesn't want to be any more involved than he has to be.'

Yeah, that's what Sempronia had told me, and it was nice to have it confirmed. Speaking of which: 'Ah... He gets on well with his stepsister, does he? Sempronia?' I couldn't break a confidence, but there was no harm in fishing.

'Sure. In fact, from the way he talks about her I'd say better than well.'

'He talks about her a lot, then?'

Bellarius took a swallow of his wine before answering.

60

'No. No, he doesn't, hardly at all, which is pretty odd, really, particularly when he's so upfront where his mother and Eutacticus are concerned. But when he does... Titus isn't one for girls, Corvinus. Not that he's the other way inclined, I don't mean that at all, it's just that he takes them too seriously.' He grinned. 'Unlike me. And if he is interested in Sempronia then I don't blame him because by all accounts she's a stunner. So I don't pry, and when he gets a bit carried away over a cup or two of wine I just play dumb and change the subject. Right?'

Right. Bellarius might not know a synonym for "besotted", but *ingénu* or not the guy was no fool.

'Besides, she's engaged to Statius Liber, down in Beneventum. Which is a pity, really. I've met him – our fathers do a lot of deals together – and he's a complete prat.'

'So,' I said. 'Let's get back to these possibilities. About where he might be.'

'You could try his uncle Sextus. He heads an acting troupe, and Titus's said more than once he wouldn't mind joining up with them if things got too bad. I don't know where you'd find him, though.'

'Bacanae. I was there a couple of days ago. No luck.'

'Then I'm sorry. That was my best shot. In fact, it was my

only shot. Titus isn't really your outgoing type, he doesn't have any other relatives that I know of or even any particular friends apart from me. Certainly not one he'd ask to put him up if he left home.'

'How about enemies?' I was clutching at straws here, and I knew it. But there weren't many avenues left to explore, and that was one angle we hadn't covered.

'That's a lot easier. Publius Paetinius.'

Prompt. Too prompt for comfort; he hadn't even paused to think. And the tone was matter-of-fact, like the answer was obvious.

'Who's Publius Paetinius?'

'Sestia Galla's son.' I must've looked blank, because he said: 'Sestia Galla was Eutacticus's first wife. After they divorced, she married Gaius Paetinius. Bastard Publius was the happy product.'

That last bit had come out with more than a smidgeon of overtones. 'Hang on, pal,' I said. 'Okay, fair enough, there was a family connection of a sort between the two, but it doesn't explain the enemies business. Couples get divorced and remarry all the time. That doesn't mean to say the kids of the separate ménages have to be at each other's throats. Not without a reason.'

'Oh, Paetinius has a reason. Or thinks he has, anyway.

Paetinius Senior was Eutacticus's partner, in the days when he was only an up-and-coming crook and needed one. Eutacticus suspected Sestia of having an affair with him, which was why he divorced her. She was pregnant with Publius at the time, she married Paetinius a month after the divorce, and she had Publius three months later.'

'Ah.' Yeah, that would do it right enough. Jupiter! 'So Publius could've been Eutacticus's son, or he could've been Paetinius's and the reason for the divorce, right?'

'Right. It's the family scandal. Paetinius Junior hates Titus's guts because he claims there was no affair, Eutacticus divorced his mother for no reason, he's the legitimate son and Titus and his mother are scheming interlopers who've cheated him of his rights.'

'Even if Titus doesn't want anything to do with his stepfather?'

'That doesn't weigh with Paetinius. Titus has told him often enough, but he just doesn't believe him.'

'So what sort of guy is he? In himself, I mean?'

Bellarius grinned. 'I told you. He's a bastard. And not the sort you'd like to cross.'

'Anything specific happen? Between him and Titus?'

'Oh, they've come head to head now and again. Any time

63

they've met, in fact. But it didn't go beyond words, not until about two months back.'

'Tell me.'

'It was at the Elms. We were sitting at our usual table, Titus and me, when Paetinius comes up out of nowhere, canned out of his skull, picks up Titus's cup and throws the wine into his face. Just like that, no warning, nothing. Titus hauls off and hits him, Paetinius goes down like he's been filleted, and that's the end of it.'

'That was it? One punch?'

'Just the one.' Bellarius grinned again. 'You've never met Titus, Corvinus. He may be quiet, but he's a big lad who can handle his fists, and however Paetinius likes to pretend otherwise where fighting's concerned he's a talentless runt. Titus floored him completely, broke his nose and probably loosened a tooth or two. A couple of the waiters had seen the whole thing. They lugged him to the gate, dumped him outside and told him in no uncertain terms his future custom wasn't welcome. Not that he was a regular, he must've come specially to make trouble, and it served him right. The whole thing was over in a minute flat.'

Gods! I didn't like this more than half. It was probably just my conspiracy-theory thought processes that were kicking into gear, mind, but put together someone who's disappeared without trace or prior notice and another someone who had good reason to wish him in an urn and the next link in the chain of reasoning isn't too difficult. Besides, the cold feeling in my gut was telling me it was no coincidence. Maybe the guy's mother – and his girlfriend – were right to be worried.

'You know where I can find this Publius Paetinius?' I said.

'No idea.' Bellarius held out the wine jug but I shook my head: good Caecuban or not, I had things to do. 'We're not exactly on friendly terms. And I don't move in these circles.'

'Right.' I stood up. 'Thanks for your help.'

'You're welcome. Any time. When you find Titus, tell him to get in touch.'

'Sure.' I turned to go. 'The other way round as well. If not with his mother, then at least with Sempronia.'

'I'll do that. Oh, and Corvinus?'

I turned back. 'Yeah?'

'That introduction. To your wife. I'd really appreciate it. Ovidius Naso's my favourite poet, and she might be able to give me a few pointers on the *Art of Love*.'

'No problem.' At least, I hoped not. Still, if there were and I'd been wrong about the no ulterior motive side of things

after all then I was sure Perilla could handle them.
Time for another chat with Sempronia.

SIX

The slave showed me through to a sectioned-off part of
the garden with a fountain and trellised rosebushes.
Sempronia was sitting in one of a couple of wickerwork
chairs, reading, with the maid I'd seen before parked on a
marble bench behind her.

She looked up as I came over. She'd changed into a sky-
blue mantle, and her hair was tied back with a ribbon.
Taken together with the roses and the fountain, she
could've come straight off a wall painting. Not one by that
weird bastard Daistratus, either.

'Back again, Corvinus?' she said. 'Did you find Quintus
Bellarius?'

'Yeah. Yeah, I did,' I said. I pulled up the other chair and
sat down.

'Any news?'

'No, I'm afraid not. Not as such.'

She put the book-roll carefully aside on the table next to
her. 'He didn't have any ideas where Titus might've
gone? None at all?'

'I'm sorry, lady.'

'Never mind. It was worth a try.' She turned round to the
maid. 'Cleia. Go and fetch Valerius Corvinus a cup of
wine. And a fruit juice for me. Cleia!'

The girl had been sitting with her head lowered, staring at the ground. She gave a start, her head came up, and she looked at me. I caught a glimpse of reddened eyes in a puffed-up face, and then she was gone, hurrying towards the house. I looked back at Sempronia.

'She's Lynchus's girlfriend,' Sempronia said. 'He didn't tell her he and Titus were leaving, either. Things have been...fraught.'

'Ah.'

'You forget they're people too, sometimes, don't you?'

'Yeah. I suppose you do.'

'Now. If you don't have any news, Corvinus, why exactly are you here? Not that it isn't nice to see you, of course.'

'Publius Paetinius. Bellarius said he had a dust-up with Titus at the Three Elms a couple of months back.'

'Oh.' Her expression hardened.

'You knew about that?'

'Yes.'

'Care to tell me about him?'

'There isn't much to tell. Paetinius is the skeleton in the family cupboard. I suppose Bellarius told you why?'

'More or less, yeah.'

'Then I can't add much. Certainly not to give you the truth of the matter, because I was only eighteen months old

68

when my father divorced my mother. Paetinius claims to be father's son, and he hates Titus. Personally, I've never met him, and from what I know of him from Titus I've no wish to.'

'How about your mother? You ever see her?'

'No. After the divorce, father severed all connection. It may sound dreadful to you, Corvinus, but I don't even think of her as my mother. I never have, and I've certainly no memories of her that might lead me to. Sestia Galla's just a name.'

'So you don't know where she lives?'

'Somewhere on the Esquiline. I don't know exactly. Is it important?'

'It's an avenue worth checking.'

I'd kept my voice carefully neutral, but Sempronia was no fool. She flashed me a look.

'You think Paetinius might have something to do with Titus's disappearance?' she said.

'Probably not. Still, it wouldn't do any harm to have a word with the guy.'

'No. No, I suppose it wouldn't. And as you said it's something worth checking.' She was quiet for a moment. 'Corvinus, Titus is all right, isn't he? I mean, you will find him, he's just gone off somewhere, hasn't he?'

'Sure he has, lady. Nothing to worry about, I'm just looking at all the angles.' Yeah, right; I wished I was as certain as I sounded, but it was what she needed to hear and there was no point in ringing alarm bells before I had to.

'Yes. Yes, of course you are. You have to, I suppose. And Critias will know Sestia Galla's address.'

'Critias?'

'Our major-domo, and has been since before I was born. We can ask him.'

'Fine.'

The maid was back, carrying a tray with the two cups on it.

'Just set it down,' Sempronia said to her. 'Then go back inside. Tell Critias that Valerius Corvinus needs Sestia Galla's address.'

The maid gave me another quick glance, then ducked her head and left without a word.

'So what now?' Sempronia said.

'I wish I knew, lady. Frankly, our best bet is that he gets in touch with you direct. Or with someone, anyway. Otherwise I'm afraid we're stuck. Unless you've got some more ideas yourself?'

She shook her head. 'I've thought and thought. Believe

me, if there was the remotest chance of pointing you in a useful direction then I'd do it. But there isn't one. Honestly. All I can say is that none of this is in the least like Titus. He'd never leave like that without telling me, never. Nor would Lynchus, where Cleia's concerned.'

'You're sure he didn't mention anything either? Lynchus, I mean?'

'Absolutely. Cleia would've said. You can ask her yourself, if you like, but she doesn't know any more than I do. And as you've seen she's as worried as I am.' She lowered her eyes, then went on quietly: 'Because I am worried, Corvinus. Yes, I know it's silly, that they're both perfectly fine, but there you are.'

I hadn't touched my wine, no more than she had her fruit juice, but I reckoned that, top-grade Falernian though it no doubt was, I'd give it a miss: I'm no hypocrite, and where offering reassurances I didn't believe myself was concerned I'd already shot my bolt. I stood up.

'Yeah, well,' I said. 'You never know, something may turn up. Meanwhile if your major-domo can give me Sestia Galla's address I can talk to Paetinius, see what he has to say.'

'Yes.' She stood up too. 'Thank you. I'll see you out.'

*   *   *

I'd still got a fair slice of the day left, and the Paetinius
place turned out to be half way up Patricius Incline: not
exactly on my way home, but not too far out of it, either.
Not quite in the same league as Eutacticus's mansion on
the Pincian, but whatever business Paetinius Senior was
in nowadays it obviously paid the bills comfortably and to
spare. The door slave was sitting on the lowest step,
shooting the breeze with a friend. He looked up as I
came over.

'The young master in, pal?' I said.

'No, sir. Master Publius hasn't got back yet.'

'Back?'

'From wherever he was last night. The mistress is at
home, though, if you'd like to talk to her instead.'

'Seeing the mistress'll do me fine, then,' I said. 'Valerius
Corvinus. It's a private matter.'

'Very well, sir. I'll ask if she's free.' He got up. 'Meanwhile
if you'd like to wait in the atrium?'

'Sure.'

I did, twiddling my thumbs for the next ten minutes or so
while the house slave he passed me on to checked the
lady's current availability. Decor expensive but flashy,
and the room was dominated by a huge mural featuring a
respectful Mercury assisting a plump-faced, self-satisfied-

looking guy dressed as Hercules heavenward to where a fair selection of the pantheon was waiting to greet him with knuckled forelocks. The master of the house himself, no doubt, allegorically transmogrified. Evidently modesty wasn't one of Paetinius Senior's failings. Nor, for that matter, was subtlety.

'Valerius Corvinus?'

I turned round. Sestia Galla had been a looker in her time, which came as no surprise since Sempronia had had to get it from somewhere, and Eutacticus was a non-runner. The word 'imposing' comes to mind: the lady could've modelled for Juno in the mural. Also, she was dressed to the nines, made up and coiffeured to the eyeballs, and was hung with enough jewellery to kit out half of the Saepta.

'You wanted to see me. What about?' Careful vowels: I'd bet you wouldn't have to scratch the surface too hard to reach an accent that was pure something else.

'It's, uh, personal,' I said. 'Not to say delicate.'

'Really? Then you'd better sit down.'

I did, on one of the couches. She took a chair. 'Your daughter gave me your address. Sempronia.'

'Did she, indeed?' The temperature dropped several notches. 'I wasn't aware that she even knew it.'

'She's worried about her stepbrother. Titus Luscius. He's disappeared, and I'm trying to find him for her.'

She stood up. 'Valerius Corvinus, let me say now, once and for all, that I have no connection with that family. Particularly that side of it. If your reason for coming here is concerned with them, then I think you should go.'

I didn't move. 'I understand your son had a quarrel with young Luscius in a wineshop about two months back. To do with...well, let's just say it was to do with inheritance.'

If looks could kill, then the one I got from Sestia Galla was the sort of hatchet-job that leaves blood on the walls. 'Are you accusing Publius of having something to do with Luscius's disappearance?' she snapped.

'No. Nothing like that. But before I go any further I thought it was only fair to get the other side of the story.'

'Publius has been treated shamefully. We both have. If he shows his resentment in a practical way then he has every right to do so. And I do not think, Valerius Corvinus, that it is any of your business, as certainly the disappearance of that young man is none of mine. Now leave my house, please, before I have you thrown out of it.'

Yeah, well; maybe it had been a mistake coming, at that. I stood up. 'Thank you for your help, Sestia Galla. If you –

,

– which was when the young guy came into the atrium
from the lobby. He was about twenty years old, and he
was wearing what was left of a party-mantle and wreath.
When he saw me he stopped.

Evidently the wayward son and heir.

'Who're you?' he said. Slurred.

'His name's Valerius Corvinus, dear.' Sestia Galla shot
him a nervous glance. 'He's just leaving.'

'You're Publius, right?' I said. 'Good party?'

'Probably. Can't remember.' He threw himself down on
the nearest couch, and his wreath slipped off and fell to
the floor. Roses and ivy leaves: if the leaves were
supposed to ward off drunkenness then they were doing
a pretty poor job, because he was stewed to the gills.

'You didn't happen to see Titus Luscius there, did you?'

He raised his head and goggled at me. 'That bastard?
Why should he be there?'

'Just asking. Seen him recently at all?'

'Publius, dear, I think you should go upstairs,' his mother
said, then gave me a look that could've come straight off
a glacier. 'Corvinus, you get out, please. Now.'

'Okay, lady. Just going, no problem.' I hadn't moved.
'Well?' I said to Publius.

He was still goggling. Finally, he said: 'I haven't seen him for months, if you want to know. Not since he broke my nose. And if I do I'll do the same to him or worse. Now piss off like my mother told you or I'll throw you out myself.'

Yeah, right. I gave him my best smile, resisted the urge to give him a finger as well, and made for the door.

Home.

SEVEN

Bathyllus was waiting with the obligatory cup of wine.

'The mistress around, little guy?' I said after the first swallow.

'Yes, sir. She's in the dining room. With the' – he paused – '*artist.*'

Oh, hell. No love lost there, evidently: there was more raw poison squeezed into that last word than could've been mustered on a good day by a dozen Egyptian asps working their little socks off. Not that I was surprised. I went through, taking the wine cup with me.

'Oh, hello, dear.' Perilla was looking flustered. 'I didn't expect you back so early. This is Daistratus. Daistratus, my husband.'

Jupiter! Artistic giant the guy might be, but as phrases go you didn't get much more metaphorical. I estimated his height as four foot nothing in his sandals. Given that the sandals had extra-thick soles and he stood up straight enough.

'Honoured to meet you, Valerius Corvinus,' he said. From the tone he obviously thought it should be the other way round. My sympathies were with Bathyllus already.

'Yeah,' I said, teeth firmly gritted. We shook, while Perilla watched us anxiously.

'Daistratus is just finishing the blocking-in,' she said.
'Then he'll make a start on the painting itself.'

'Fine, fine.' I made the mistake of glancing at the thing,
but managed to wrench my eyes away before my brain
could kick into gear and start trying to interpret what they
were seeing. 'It's certainly...different.'

The artistic giant puffed up like a partridge. 'Of course it
is different!' he said. 'It is *unique*!'

'So what about the other six?'

'I beg your pardon?'

'This is, uh, Fantasy Architecturecrap Seven, yes?'

'Scape. Architecture*scape*.'

'Right. Sorry, pal, slip of the tongue. So what about
versions one to six?'

'They are different too. And equally unique.'

'Completely different, or just slightly different? Because if
they're just slightly different then that only makes them
slightly unique, right? Which is sort of a contradiction in
terms. I mean, if the only difference in the name is the
number tacked onto the end, then –'

'Marcus,' Perilla said, taking me by the arm, 'perhaps we
should leave Daistratus alone to work in peace, yes?'
She edged me towards the door.

'It's a reasonable point, lady. I mean, we are paying for

the thing. Have paid, rather. If it's supposed to be unique and half a dozen other lucky people have practically the same picture on their wall –'

'*Marcus!*' she hissed. The edging got a lot more insistent. You could've used the glare I was getting from the Artist Known as Daistratus to weld metal.

'Fair enough. See you later, friend,' I said to him. 'Keep up the good…ah…keep up the work, okay?'

We went back into the atrium, Perilla maintaining an arm-lock and a frigid silence throughout.

'If that guy's having it off with Rutilia Secunda then he'll need a stepladder and a bit of help,' I said. Rutilia was the poetry-klatsch pal who'd given Perilla the recommendation in the first place. She stood six feet one in her socks and was built like an all-in wrestler.

'Don't be crude,' Perilla snapped.

'Yeah, well.' I lay down on the couch and set the wine cup on the table. There again, maybe I was doing the woman an injustice. I doubted that Daistratus would have much on his mind beyond his art. If you could call it that.

'So. How was your morning?' Spoken with careful deliberation; we'd obviously reached an obligatory change of subject here. Which was fine by me. I took another swallow of wine and told her.

'You think this Paetinius has something to do with the boy's disappearance?'

'It's possible. Everything's possible. I hope not, though. The time to work along these lines is when we find the corpse.' I made the sign against bad luck. 'Sorry, lady. That slipped out.'

'Will there be one? A corpse, I mean?'

'Perilla, I don't know. Honestly. Young Luscius has just disappeared, that's all. We've no reason to think he's dead, quite the reverse, because he walked out of the place of his own accord. It's just a question of finding where he is, and that's difficult enough.'

'You've no leads? None?'

'Not a sniff.' I finished off the Setinian and set the cup down. 'My best bet's that he'll get in touch with his girlfriend. Although where that leaves me vis-à-vis Eutacticus is another matter, because I doubt if sweet Sempronia's likely to share the information with her daddy. Or her stepmother either, to tell the truth. She might not even tell me. I mean, why should she?'

'So what are you going to do?'

'Sit tight. Wait. Keep my fingers crossed. And if Eutacticus loses patience watch my back.'

'That's scarcely fair, dear. You've tried your best.'

'That bastard doesn't do fair. He's known for it.'

'Then have a word with one of the city judges and let Eutacticus know you've done it. He wouldn't dare interfere with you then.'

I sighed. 'Perilla, there's a good chance that whoever I talked to got to be a judge in the first place because Eutacticus chipped in to fund his election campaign. Or maybe he just has the guy and his wife round to dinner regularly and pulls out all the stops, or gets them prime seats at the Games. That sort of thing. Nothing too obvious, but he's a top-level professional crook, and he's good at his job. He knows if you want a blind eye turned you have to pay for it, and he's got enough to do that ten times over. So me, I wouldn't place any bets.'

'Hmm.' Perilla frowned. 'Well, as you say we'll just have to await developments.'

*   *   *

We got them the next morning. In spades. Sempronia sent a skivvy round to say that the bodies had been found.

EIGHT

They were lying inside one of those artificial grottoes
sacred to Pan and the Nymphs that you get in the bigger
gardens, tucked away in a carefully-landscaped patch of
wilderness and screened by ivy, ferns and general bosk.
If there is such a word. This particular example was right
against the rear boundary wall of the property, on the
opposite side of the house from the main gate and
backing directly onto a stretch of undeveloped hillside.
Young Titus Luscius had been stabbed through the heart.
The slave Lynchus had had his throat cut.
Shit.
The packs were stuffed into the back of the grotto. I
pulled them out to where the light was better and undid
the draw-strings. Not a lot there, even in the bigger one,
which must've been Luscius's: a cloak, a fresh tunic, a
change of underwear, that was about what you got. No
money: he would've been carrying a purse, sure, but that
must've been on his belt, and whoever had killed him had
probably taken it as a bonus. There was some blood on
the rocky floor, but not all that much, certainly not enough
to go with the slave's slit throat; that must've been done
outside.
Well, that was that. At least we knew where we were,

now. If that was any consolation, which it wasn't.

I came back out into the sunshine to where Sempronia was waiting, arms tightly hugging her chest, head turned away. A small group of slaves were standing in a huddle a few yards off, like a Greek chorus who'd discovered they were in the wrong play. Two of them were holding stretchers. I crouched down and inspected a stain on the grass to one side of the grotto entrance. Yeah, right: blood, although mostly washed away by the trickling stream of runoff water. That was where Lynchus must've been standing. There were splashes on the surrounding rocks, too, and at more or less head height on the outward-facing side of the entrance. Easy enough to spot, but only if you were looking for them.

Sempronia must've heard me. 'Stasimus found them,' she said, without turning round. 'He's one of the garden slaves. He had a...an assignation with one of the maids here, just before dawn.'

Her voice was colourless, but the tone was matter-of-fact and she was holding herself in well. She'd been doing it ever since I'd arrived at the house, and she'd insisted on taking me to the grotto herself. Like I said, Eutacticus's daughter was no fluffy kitten. The best thing I could do was match her.

'Was there any reason for Titus to come here?' I said. 'I mean, any special reason that you know of?'

She turned. 'Yes. It was where we met, when we wanted to be together. Where we arranged to meet. No one ever comes to this part of the garden, especially at this time of year.'

'Uh-huh.' Well, that made sense. And, of course, it explained why this Stasimus had chosen it for his own clandestine amorous activities. 'Anyone know about that?'

'No.' She shrugged. 'Or not that I'm aware of. We were very careful. But it's not impossible.'

Right. And it could just be coincidence. The rest of the grounds were fairly open, flower beds and the like. The grotto would be the perfect place to choose for a private meeting of any kind, particularly when there were going to be bodies involved at the end of it. If you knew it was there, that is.

'Ah...you happen to know if your father's accountant is around this morning?' I said neutrally. 'Astrapton?'

Not neutrally enough. Sempronia was no fool. She shot me a look.

'Probably,' she said. 'I'll send one of the slaves to find out.'

'No, that's OK. I'll go myself.'

'Then I'll come with you.'

'You sure?'

'Yes. Oh, yes. Very sure.' She took a deep breath. 'Have you finished here, Valerius Corvinus? With the...with Titus, I mean.'

I nodded. She turned to the slaves. 'Carry them into the house,' she said. 'Carefully, please. Critias has made the arrangements. He'll tell you where to put them.'

The slaves unrolled the stretchers. We left them to it and walked back towards the house in silence. Sempronia didn't look back at the grotto. Or at me.

'If it was Astrapton who did it,' she said eventually, 'I'll have him crucified. And if I can I'll hammer the nails in myself.'

Ouch! 'We can't be sure that he's the killer,' I said. 'He lied about seeing them leave, but that's as far as it goes. What reason would he have?'

'I don't know. But the lie is enough. If he won't explain that now to me then my father'll persuade him otherwise. He's very good at persuasion.'

My stomach went cold. *No fluffy kitten* was right, in spades. Sempronia was no girl to cross.

We went inside and through the house to the annexe

where the accountant had his office. The cubby-hole was empty. Without a word, Sempronia led me to the clerks' room further along the corridor where four or five slaves were working. They looked up startled as we came in.

'Where's Astrapton?' she said.

'In a meeting with the master, miss,' one of the slaves said.

'He know anything about the finding of young Master Titus's body earlier this morning?' I asked.

That got me a nervous look. 'Yes, sir. Of course. We all do.'

Par for the course: nothing escapes the slave grapevine for long. Sure, the bastard might be with Eutacticus. And pigs might fly. In any case, it would be easy enough to check.

We left them staring.

*   *   *

Eutacticus was in his own office, sitting behind his desk. Alone. For a guy who'd just lost a stepson he looked pretty normal, but then paroxysms of grief were clearly something else he didn't do. That and allow a little thing like a murder in the family to interrupt his business duties. The bastard wasn't even wearing mourning.

'Well?' he said.

'Where's Astrapton, Father?' Sempronia asked.

Eutacticus put down the pen he was holding. 'In his office, presumably,' he said. 'Why?'

'The clerks seem to think that he came here. For a meeting.'

'No. I haven't seen him since yesterday. And there was certainly no meeting arranged. What's this about?'

'The chances are he's done a runner,' I said.

'We think he killed Titus,' said Sempronia.

Eutacticus stared at us. '*Astrapton?* That's nonsense. Why the hell would Astrapton want to kill Titus?'

'Yeah, well, it's just a possibility at present,' I said. 'Still, the guy lied to me about seeing him and his slave leave the house the morning they disappeared. And now he's gone missing himself.'

Eutacticus got up, went to the door, opened it, and yelled: '*Critias!*' Then he turned back to me. 'You're sure about that?' he said.

'Like your daughter said. The boys in his department told us he was here with you. He isn't. And he knew the bodies'd been found. What do you think?'

'I don't know at present, Corvinus. But if he has disappeared, and he was involved in Titus's murder, then –'

'Yes, sir.' The major-domo. Critias.

'Go down to the gate. Don't send someone, go yourself. I want to know if Astrapton has gone out this morning, and I want a definite answer brought back within the next two minutes. Clear?'

'Yes, sir.' Critias turned to go.

'And, Critias -'

'Yes, sir?'

'If he hasn't already left then make sure he doesn't. He's to be found and brought to me.'

'Certainly, sir.' The major-domo left. Where insouciance was concerned, Bathyllus couldn't've done it better.

Eutacticus went back to his chair behind the desk. 'Right, Corvinus. Sit. I want to talk to you. Sempronia, lose yourself. This is no place for women.'

'But, Father -'

'*Go!*'

I thought she might stand her ground, but she left without a word, closing the door behind her. I pulled up a chair and sat down.

'Right, Corvinus,' Eutacticus said. 'I'm listening. And you'd better make it good, because Astrapton is one of my best employees.'

I shrugged. 'Nothing else to add, pal.' He bristled, but I

ignored it. 'When I talked to Astrapton yesterday morning he told me that on the day they disappeared he'd seen your stepson and his slave leaving the premises. Unless they came back later and got themselves murdered then the guy was lying. As to why he'd want to do that, let alone murder them himself, I've got no more idea than you have. So get off my back, right?'

I thought I'd gone too far, because Eutacticus's face had set hard and his hands on the desk-top balled into fists. Then he nodded.

'All right,' he said. 'Fair enough. Then I'll settle for your theories.'

'No theories as yet. Just questions.'

'Namely?'

'For a start, I'm assuming that Titus being dead changes the rules of the game. The hands-off business on your part. Am I right?'

He was quiet for a long time. Then he said: 'Look, Corvinus, we didn't get on, my stepson and me. Occusia's probably told you. But he was mine. Part of my family until I said different, whatever his thoughts on the matter were, and no one messes with my family and gets away with it. You understand?'

I nodded. *Mine.* That about summed the cold bastard up.

Still, I needed him behind me, and the kid himself was out of it now.

'So I'll help you all I can. You just have to ask, whatever it is, whatever it costs, you ask and it'll happen. In return, I expect you to find my stepson's killer. Just that. *Expect*, not just *want*. Deal?'

Shit. Well, it was the best I was going to get. 'Deal,' I said.

'Good.' He leaned back in his chair. 'Now. Second question.'

'Why would Astrapton want to kill your stepson? Or see him dead, or cover up for his killer? Any and all of these?'

'I told you. I can't answer that. No reason, as far as I know. Titus didn't involve himself in the business, didn't want to get involved. He and Astrapton had nothing at all to do with each other.'

'Okay. Leave Astrapton out of it for the moment. Who else would want him dead? What about young Publius Paetinius?'

That got me a look. 'Who told you about Paetinius?'

'A friend of Titus's.' I wasn't going to bring Sempronia in, if I could manage not to. That aspect of things I'd keep to myself for the present, and if Eutacticus did get to know about it then it would have to come from the lady herself.

'He a possibility?'

'He hated Titus's guts, certainly. But it's a long way from hating someone's guts to murdering them.'

Yeah. True. Still... 'Anyone else?'

'No.' Eutacticus gave me his crocodile's smile. 'Where enemies are concerned, Corvinus, if we were talking about me, if I'd been the one lying out there, I could give you a suspect list as long as your arm. But Titus...no, there's no one else.'

Right. Even so, that little speech had suggested another line of possibilities that I hadn't thought of up until then. However, that one could wait. 'Fine. Then let's try a completely different angle. Tell me about Astrapton himself.'

'How do you mean?'

'He your ex-slave or did you bring him in from outside?'

'The second. He's been with me for just under five years.' Eutacticus was frowning. 'What's this got to do with Titus? I told you, there was no connection.'

'Nothing directly. I'm just fishing for ideas. Suppose –'

There was a knock on the door and Critias came in.

'The gate slave says that Astrapton went through about half an hour ago, sir,' he said.

Eutacticus swore. 'He say where he was going?'

'No, sir. But he turned in the direction of town, and he seems to have been in a particular hurry.'

'Put the word out. I want that bastard found and brought back. That's top priority.'

'Yes, sir.' Critias left, closing the door behind him.

'So that's that, Corvinus. You were right, he's done a runner.' Eutacticus swore again. 'Don't worry, we'll get him, I promise you that. Now. What were you saying?'

'Yeah. Just suppose Astrapton's taking off *didn't* have anything to do with Titus's death. Or not directly, anyway. What other reason could he have?'

'That's obvious. It would be where any accountant was concerned. He'd been fiddling the books and knew he'd been caught.'

'Had he?'

'Not to my knowledge. But Astrapton is a sharp cookie, the best accountant I've ever had. More, he oversees the incomings and outgoings over the whole stretch of my business dealings, so he'd have a lot of scope. And as long as he wasn't too greedy he could get away with it, barring a detailed audit. Which is what's going to be arranged before the day's out, whether we find the bastard or not.'

'Fine. Meanwhile: he got any weaknesses that you know

of?'

'Weaknesses?'

'Women. Boys. Gambling. That sort of thing. Things that if they got known about, or got out of hand, could lead him into trouble.'

Eutacticus frowned. 'We talking blackmail here?'

'Something like that. Anything like that, really. I said, I'm just fishing for ideas. You tell me.'

'Women or boys I don't know. Probably the first, if anything. I do know he likes to gamble, but then he's a Greek, what do you expect? As long as he does it with his own money that's fine with me.'

Well, it wasn't much of a strand to follow up, but it was better than nothing. Certainly if Astrapton didn't have a direct reason for muddying the waters re young Titus's disappearance then being leaned on by the guilty third party was a viable motive. 'You care to amplify?' I said.

'"Amplify?"'

'Names of friends with a similar hobby? His favourite bookie? Clubs he frequents? That sort of thing.'

'I don't know offhand myself. But I'll find out. And believe me, Corvinus, if the information is there then you'll have it. That I absolutely guarantee.'

Yeah; I could believe that; Eutacticus had ways of asking

questions that I didn't even like to think about. At least now he was on my side. Or claimed to be, anyway.

I stood up. 'Fair enough,' I said. 'You know where to find me. Any developments, just send a skivvy.'

I went downstairs. They'd laid young Titus out in the atrium, his feet towards the floor; not the slave, of course, he'd be elsewhere. I cut off my token scrap of hair, put it in the basket provided, and burned a pinch of incense on the small brazier beside the funeral couch.

Then I set off home.

NINE

Perilla was upstairs in her study slaving over her anapaests. Or whatever compositional metre she was currently into. Me, unless the annual accounts are involved, when I need to use the desk space for laying out the tablets and catching the torn-out clumps of hair, I like to be comfortable, which means I loll around on a couch with a handy table next to it for the wine cup; the lady is definitely the sitting-up-straight-at-a-desk type. So that's where she was. I gave her the usual back-home kiss, carried my cup over to the rarely-used reading couch and lolled.

She closed the note-tablet and put down her pen.

'So,' she said. 'You have your bodies.'

'Yeah. Unfortunately. Be careful what you wish for, right?' I gave her the run-down.

'And you think this Astrapton was responsible?' she said when I'd finished.

'Give me a chance, lady! I don't know! It looks that way at present, sure, or at least that he was seriously involved. The problem is that he didn't have a smidgeon of motive. Direct motive, anyway. He didn't have much in the way of opportunity, either. These little details aside, the guy's perfect.'

'How do you mean, no opportunity? He lived in the same house as Luscius.'

I sighed and picked up the winecup. 'Okay,' I said. 'You're Astrapton. You've decided, for whatever reason, to kill your boss's stepson. You want to lure your victim to an out-of-the-way part of the garden. Trouble is, he's never had anything to do with you and doesn't want to, so he's hardly likely to agree to a meeting. Also, time's short, because he's heading for the tall timber. How do you do it?'

'Ah.'

'"Ah" is right.' I took a smug swig of the wine.

'Actually, I can think of three possibilities.'

I almost choked. '*What?*'

'Theoretical ones, at least.'

Jupiter! 'Theoretical's fine with me. Go ahead. The floor is yours.'

'First. You say that Luscius and Sempronia used the grotto as a meeting-place, and that she couldn't be absolutely certain that no one else knew this. If Astrapton did, then what was to stop him writing a note purporting to come from her arranging to meet at the grotto, and passing it on to Luscius?'

'He'd smell a rat straight off. He'd know she wouldn't use

Astrapton as a courier.'

'There are other ways. Astrapton is resident in the house, yes?'

'Yeah, I assume so.'

'Then it wouldn't be beyond possibility for him to, say, slip the note under Luscius's bedroom door during the night. Naturally I don't know the layout of the house itself and where the bedrooms are located in respect of one another, so that might not be feasible in practice. But the principle holds good. If the meeting was timed for before dawn, or slightly after, there would be no chance of the deception being discovered before it was too late. And it'd explain why Luscius didn't arrange to say goodbye to Sempronia and tell her where he was going. As far as he was concerned, an arrangement to meet had already been made, by Sempronia herself.'

'Would Astrapton have known her handwriting? He'd've had to, to forge a note.'

Perilla shrugged. 'Again, I don't know. Possibly, possibly not; I said, it's only a theory, to be modified by the facts. But in any case I doubt if Luscius would be unduly suspicious. After all, why should he be? As far as he knew, the relationship was still a secret, one or two words would be enough, and they needn't've included a signature. In fact, they probably wouldn't, for safety's sake. So unless the forgery was crude in the extreme Luscius wouldn't've given it a second glance.'

I grinned. 'Okay, Aristotle. As a theory, it has definite possibilities. I'll grant you that. File for reference. Next.'

'You're assuming that Astrapton did the arranging.'

'So?'

'What if he didn't? What if the meeting was Luscius's idea? Or at least that he wanted it to happen?'

'Gods, Perilla! Why should Titus Luscius want to talk to Astrapton? I said: he wouldn't even give the guy the time of day.'

'As far as you know.'

'Yeah, well, that's sort of axiomatic, isn't it? Everyone says he'd have nothing to do with his stepfather's business associates, even his mother and his girlfriend. That's enough proof for me.'

'Yes, but what if Luscius had found out somehow that Astrapton was fiddling the books, and wanted to face him with it? Perhaps attempt a little blackmail?'

'We don't know yet that Astrapton *was* on the fiddle.'

'No. But it's a strong possibility, isn't it?'

'You're fantasising, lady. One, unless I've got him completely wrong, Luscius was no blackmailer. He wasn't the type. And two, if his motive wasn't personal profit then why should he care if Astrapton was ripping Eutacticus off? From his point of view it'd simply be one crook stealing from another.'

'All right. I admit that that scenario is the most unlikely. Leave it. Third theory, also involving the blackmail theme. What if it was the other way round, and Astrapton was blackmailing Luscius?'

'Over what? Titus Luscius wasn't –' I stopped. Shit. I'd been going to say that Luscius wasn't the blackmailer's-victim type, that he wasn't the sort to have a guilty secret. But he did have one, didn't he? If Astrapton knew about the grotto then he must've known about his relationship with Sempronia, and as a top-notch accountant he could calculate how many beans made five. Yeah; that would work, and Occusia had said money wasn't a problem for her son, that Eutacticus gave him as much as he liked.

'It still wouldn't make sense, though,' I said. 'A blackmailer doesn't kill his victim. If anything, it happens the other way round.'

'Perhaps he didn't originally intend to. Perhaps Luscius was planning to kill him and Astrapton turned the tables.'

Gods! It was usually me who went out on a limb with theorising! 'Perilla, Luscius wasn't the type to commit a murder any more than he was capable of blackmail. Trust me; he wouldn't've set up a meeting intending to kill Astrapton in cold blood, no way. And if he had then that's the way things would have gone. Luscius was a big lad, he could handle himself in a fight, we know that from his pal Bellarius. Besides, there was the slave Lynchus as well. If it had come to an actual fight, particularly if he'd been taken by surprise, a weed like Astrapton wouldn't've stood a chance.'

'But he evidently did. If it was him. More than a chance. The murder victims were Luscius and his slave, not Astrapton.'

I frowned. 'Yeah. That's been puzzling me. Oh, one person could've done both murders, no argument, but to keep the element of surprise he'd have to have been sure of taking the pair down one at a time. Plus he'd have to be up to the job, because if he fumbled either killing, particularly the first one, the chances are he'd be up shit creek. Certainly scratch the surprise element.'

'So?'

'So I think Astrapton – if it was Astrapton – had an accomplice. Things'd be a lot easier with two people.'

'You mean someone from inside the house?'

'No. Not necessarily, in fact not at all. The boundary wall

backs directly onto the hill. There's plenty of rough cover the other side, so any third party'd have all the time he needed to get over with zero risk of being spotted. He could even've used a ladder. And an accomplice would fit the mechanics of the thing. Astrapton takes Luscius inside leaving the slave to keep watch so they can discuss their business in private. Meanwhile his pal hidden in the shrubbery slits Lynchus's throat – that was done just outside the entrance to the grotto, I saw the bloodstains – and then comes in to help Astrapton kill Luscius. That make sense?'

Perilla was twisting a lock of hair. 'Yes, Marcus, it does. And it would fit in just as well with the first theory of the bogus note. So if we shelve the question of motive for the present then who would the accomplice have been?'

'Easy. Young Paetinius. Oh, it's just a guess, but we don't have any other front runners and he's a fair bet. It'd solve the problem of motive, too, because Paetinius had it in spades, and from what Luscius's pal Bellarius told me he has the form as well.' I took a swallow of the wine. 'It all fits beautifully. Paetinius makes the running and sets up the plan, Astrapton facilitates things from the inside.'

'Just a moment. You're assuming some prior connection

between the two.'

'Yeah.' I rubbed my chin. 'True.'

'Besides, despite what you say, I'm not at all sure that even outright hatred would constitute enough of a motive to commit murder. There would have to be something more concrete, surely. And there's still the very moot question of whether Paetinius would have the intellectual capacity to plan one.'

'True again. All the same -' I stopped. Oh, gods! I'd cracked it! Or part of it, anyway… 'No there isn't. Because he didn't need to have.'

'Pardon?'

'And there was something more concrete.'

'Namely?'

'Something that Eutacticus said when I talked to him this morning. That if it'd been him – Eutacticus himself – who'd been murdered I'd have a suspect list of enemies as long as my arm. And his ex-partner would be right at the top. Paetinius senior.'

'Marcus, we're talking about the son, not the father!'

'Just hear me out. It comes to the same thing in the end, more or less. And it makes much more sense if father and son were in it together.'

'Explain.'

'If Eutacticus was planning to adopt young Luscius –
whatever the kid's own plans in that direction were – then
getting rid of the son and heir might strike the elder
Paetinius as a pretty good idea. Particularly if with
Luscius gone his own son might be in the running again
to inherit Eutacticus's business operations.'

'Now *that* is far-fetched!'

'Not as far fetched as it sounds. Whatever Eutacticus's
feelings are on the matter, young Paetinius and his
mother both claim – and maybe genuinely believe – that
they've been screwed out of their rights. Their *legal*
rights. According to Bellarius, Titus Luscius'd told
Paetinius until he was blue in the face that he had no
interest in taking over from his stepfather, and Paetinius
still didn't believe him. Now Luscius is actually dead,
whether he was only acting disinterested or not is
irrelevant. And what happens if Eutacticus dies without a
replacement heir?'

'If he can get himself recognised as Eutacticus's son
under law, then Paetinius would inherit. Could he?'

'I don't know. I'm no lawyer. But he was born only four
months after his parents' divorce, and the whole business
of Paetinius Senior being his natural father could just be
malicious gossip and suspicion on Eutacticus's part.

Certainly it can't be proved for definite, as it'd have to be for the thing to stand up in court. So, yeah, I'd reckon he's at least in with a shout. A better shout than if Luscius was still around, anyway. Particularly with the elder Paetinius's money to buy the best rep in the city and grease the legal wheels.'

'Mmm.' Perilla was still twisting her hair. 'You know, it might even provide the missing motive for Astrapton. And the prior connection.'

'How so?'

'If he had been putting in a bit of creative accountancy, it'd be sensible to have a contingency plan for the future, wouldn't it? In case he was found out eventually?'

'Sure, but –' I stopped; I'd seen where she was going. 'He gets in touch with one of the Paetinii – Senior or Junior, it doesn't matter, lump them together as an item – and tells them he might be up for involvement in any scam they have cooking where Eutacticus and his stepson are concerned, in return for a guaranteed bolt-hole if he needs it. Yeah, that might work. Well done, lady. Astrapton is definitely in the frame. To say nothing of the Paetinius family.' I stretched. 'Still, we're a long way from proof. Enough for today, leave it for now. You want some lunch?'

'No, Marcus, I really need to get on with this. It's for our next poetry meeting.'

'Yeah. Right. Well, I think I'll get Meton to make me an omelette, then take the afternoon off and go over to Renatius's to prop up the bar with the punters. Assuming nothing else transpires in the meantime.' I got up, picked up my wine cup and went to the door. 'See you later.'

One thing, though: if I was having an omelette I'd eat it off a tray in the atrium. There hadn't been any sign of our pint-sized artistic guru when I'd come in – no doubt he was sharing his prodigious talents among several lucky households and we'd just have to wait in line until he deigned to take Fantasy Architecturescape Seven to the next stage – but just knowing while I ate that that aberration in the dining room was lurking behind my back waiting to pounce would put me right off my lunch.

Ah, well, no doubt it would all work itself out; I had infinite confidence in Bathyllus's deviousness and ingenuity, and judging by his reactions so far he was not going to take this lying down. Or at worst scenario it'd be whitewash time at the earliest opportunity, and screw the money. Meanwhile it was Renatius's and an hour or two of shooting the breeze. The case could just simmer on the back boiler for a while.

TEN

I'd just finished breakfast in the garden next morning when Bathyllus oozed up with Laughing George – aka Eutacticus's principal muscle Satrius – in close attendance. On a miffed rating of one to ten, the little guy was showing a clear fifteen.

'It appears you have a visitor, sir,' he said. 'I asked him to wait in the lobby, but –'

'That's okay, Bathyllus. No harm done.' I brushed the bread-crumbs off my tunic. 'Go and count the spoons.'

'Morning, Corvinus,' Satrius said as Bathyllus huffed off. 'The boss sent me.'

'Yeah, I'd sort of guessed that.' I stood up. 'You've found Astrapton?'

'Nah, not yet. I'm taking you to the Golden Fleece.'

'What's the Golden Fleece?'

'Gambling joint. The boss said you'd asked him to find where the bastard did most of his hanging out. Word is, the Fleece. So that's where we're going.'

'Uh...isn't it a little early, pal? These places don't open until –'

'You'll be with me, Corvinus. If we want the Fleece to be open then it will be fucking open. With little blue bows on.'

Right. Right. Well, it had only been a passing observation. 'You have an address, maybe?' I said.

'Banker's Incline, behind the Porcian Hall.'

The other side of town, near the Citadel. Still, it was a good day for walking. 'Fine. I'm ready. Let's go.'

'I've got a litter outside.'

'If it's all the same to you, friend, I'd rather –'

'Look. I've walked all the way from the fucking Pincian already this morning. We take the litter, right?'

We took the litter.

* * *

Gambling's technically illegal in Rome, barring at the Winter Festival, but in practice the law's pretty much a dead letter in these more permissive days. Even so, if you provide a facility that encourages its customers to lose their shirts and hock their grandmothers outwith the comfort of their own homes, making the fact obvious is not a sharp idea. The Golden Fleece was an anonymous building in one of the blocks between the Porcian Hall and the Fontinal Gate; more specifically, a door with a heavy iron grille set between a cutler's shop and a bakery. Satrius waited while I paid off the litter – evidently transporting purple-stripers didn't come under the heading of legitimate expenses where gorillas were concerned – and knocked.

A face appeared at the grille. 'Bugger off,' it said. 'We're closed.' Then it saw Satrius and did a double-take. 'Ah. There again –'

There was a rattling of bolts and the door opened to reveal a weedy slave in a threadbare tunic, clutching a mop like it was some apotropaic talisman. We went in. 'Cicirrus around?' Satrius said.

'Yes, sir. In the office.' The slave swallowed nervously. 'It's through here. If you'd like to follow me, sir.'

We did. Separating punters from their money, or creaming off a percentage, however places like that did things, was obviously a lucrative business. The Golden Fleece was done up like a top-grade cathouse, which it may well have doubled as: gilt candelabra, inlaid cedar tables, couches upholstered in red velvet with gold tassel edging, and pricey artwork on the walls, particularly the centrepiece with a seriously-hung Jason heading for the tall timber clutching the eponymous fleece with one hand and a well-endowed Medea with the other. The lady appeared to have lost most of her clothes in the spat with the dragon and was in the process of rapidly losing the rest of them. Well, where subject matter was concerned it beat fantasy architecture hands down, that was for sure.

The slave took us through the main room to a door at the back. He knocked, opened it and stepped aside. The guy behind the desk looked up from the tablets he was working on: late middle-age, balding, a run to fat that was more of a bolt.

'This'd better be important,' he snapped, 'because if it isn't –' He stopped, did a double-take, and swallowed, just like the slave had done. I was beginning to see a definite pattern forming here. 'Ah. Satrius. Not a problem, is there?'

'Nah. Least, I hope not. The boss just needs some information, is all.'

'Of course. Anything I can do to help.'

'This is Valerius Corvinus. He's got some questions for you. The boss wants you to answer them. No fudging, no cover-ups, just the straight answers. Okay?'

'Certainly.' Cicirrus gave me a nervous look. 'About what?'

'A guy by the name of Astrapton,' I said. 'He comes here quite often, doesn't he?'

Cicirrus swallowed again, and his face took on a faintly greenish tinge. 'Yes,' he said. 'Astrapton's one of our regulars. What about him?'

'You know he's Eutacticus's accountant?'

'Ah...yes. Yes, I did understand something to that effect.'

'So how's he been doing lately? Wins and losses? In the red or the black?'

'You mean "lately", lately?' His eyes shifted. 'Neither one nor the other, really. Middle-of-the-road. He might be up or down a few hundred over the course of an evening, but –'

'I told you, pal,' Satrius said. 'And I only tell people once. No fudging.'

'Look, the house only takes a percentage, right?' Cicirrus was definitely green now. 'We only provide the venue, we don't set the stakes or the limits. That's the clients' own business.'

'Understood,' I said. 'Now tell me what you're not telling me.'

Cicirrus licked his lips. 'He went through a bad patch about six months ago that put him twenty thousand down at least. Probably a good bit more, I don't know exactly. But he paid it off. Or at least, his creditors seem to be perfectly happy with things. Certainly I've heard no more about it, and he's still a client in good standing.'

I blinked: twenty thousand plus was serious, serious gravy. And not the sort of money that a freedman accountant could come up with in a hurry. Not out of his own pocket, anyway. We'd got the bastard. 'Can you let me have a list of the creditors concerned, and where I can reach them?' I said. 'That possible?'

'Yes. Yes, of course.' He was sweating now. He reached for a blank tablet and a pen and started scribbling frantically. We waited. Finally, he handed the tablet over to me. 'There you are. I think that's all of them.'

'You had better be fucking sure about that, pal,' Satrius said. 'Because if we find out that it isn't –'

'It is! All of them! I swear!'

I glanced at the tablet. Four names. None of them meant anything to me, but I passed the tablet over to Satrius. He read it, his lips moving. Yeah, well: the guy had other, more germane professional qualities. Like the ability to intimidate the shit out of our sweating friend here. Those four names would be all there were, I was sure of that.

'Any bells?' I said.

'Nah. They're just ordinary punters, far as I can see.' Satrius handed the tablet back to me. 'Okay, Cicirrus, that's it for the present. But the boss'll expect you to drop round for a chat in the very near future. About how his accountant could run up a debt of twenty thousand and then pay it off without you letting him know. Understand?'

Cicirrus's Adam's apple worked its way up and down. 'Of

course. It'll be a pleasure.'

Satrius grinned. 'I doubt that, sunshine. But see it happens, okay? And if there's anything else you feel like telling him in the meantime, don't hesitate to get in touch.'

'I will certainly do that.'

'Fine.' He glanced at me. 'You finished, Corvinus? Got all you wanted?'

'Sure.'

'Then I'll be getting back. You can find your own way home?'

Jupiter! Don't tell me the guy was metamorphosing into some sort of horrendous baby-minder. 'Yeah,' I said. 'Yeah, I think that I could just about manage that. So long as you point me in the right direction.'

Satrius grunted, and left. I left, too, but not directly for home: the man at the top of the list lived near Pearlmarket Porch, which was almost on the way back to the Caelian. While I was in this part of town I reckoned I might as well drop in on him and see what his story was.

* * *

'Would that be Sextilius Acceptus Senior or Junior, sir?' the door-slave said when I asked if the guy was at home. 'Uh...I'm not sure, pal,' I said. 'It's about a gambling debt.'

The slave gave a sniff that was pure Bathyllus. 'Junior,

then. I'm not sure if he's up yet. Your name, sir?'

I told him.

'Very well. If you'd care to wait in the lobby I'll find out.'

He went off to do that small thing while I kicked my heels in the Sextilii-Accepti-plural lobby. Evidently unshaven strangers - I hadn't had a chance to get round to that before Laughing George had shown up - calling on the subject of the son and heir's gambling debts didn't rate the atrium. Not that the slave had shown much surprise.

The slave came back. 'He'll be down in a moment, sir. If you'd like to come through to the study.'

It took considerably longer than a moment, but Acceptus the Younger finally crept in. *Crept* being the operative word: if I knew a hangover when I saw it - and I did, believe me, from when I was this kid's age - then this one was a beaut, the full don't-speak-too-loudly-because-my-head'll-fall-off catastrophe.

'What did you say your name was?' he said.

'Corvinus. Valerius Corvinus.'

'Never seen you before in my life.' He frowned. 'Have I?'

'No.'

'So what's this about a gambling debt?'

'It's not to me, pal. And I'm not putting the bite on. All I want is some information.'

The frown vanished; he looked relieved. 'About what?'

'You know a guy by the name of Astrapton?'

'Yeah, I know Gaius Astrapton. We play together regularly at the Fleece, us and a few friends.'

'When did you last see him?'

'A couple of days ago. He took a cool hundred off me.'

'He, uh, reliable? Where money's concerned?'

'Sure, he's reliable.' The frown was back. 'We wouldn't cut him in if he wasn't. What's this about? He owe you money?'

'No. But I was told that he took a real pasting about six months back. Twenty thousand plus.'

'Yeah, that's so. Twenty five, as a matter of fact. What business is it of yours?'

'And that he settled the debt in full. I was just wondering where the money came from.'

Acceptus chuckled. 'You saying you think it wasn't his?'

'It's a possibility. I'm looking into things for his boss.'

'His *boss?*'

'Yeah. Anything strange about that?'

'It's news to me, that's all. I didn't know he had a boss. Oh, he's a freedman, sure, but I thought he had a business in his own right. A pretty thriving one, at that, import and export.'

'Is that so, now?'

'Sure. Not that he said so, in so many words, but that was the impression I got. That we all got. We didn't ask outright. House etiquette: so long as he pays his way and settles his debts, outwith the Fleece a guy's private life is his own affair. If he wants to keep it quiet, that's his concern.' He was frowning again. 'You're saying Astrapton's been on the take? Dipping his hands in the till?'

'So it would seem. He settle the debt in cash?'

'Cash money, as ever is, silver piece for silver piece. No quibbles, no delays. So where is he now?'

'I don't know. He's disappeared, and his boss is looking for him.'

'Jupiter! You live and learn.' Acceptus shook his head, then winced and shuddered. 'He was okay, Astrapton. He was good company, and like I said he settled his debts. That was a once-off, he just hit an unlucky streak, happens to us all. So what was his boss's name?'

'Don't worry about it, pal.' I was already heading for the door. 'Thanks for your help. I'll see myself out.'

*　*　*

So. We'd got our proof. Forget the Caelian; I needed to have another talk with Eutacticus.

ELEVEN

Eutacticus hit the desk with his fist, hard. 'The bastard!
The scheming, two-timing, treacherous *bastard!*'

Yeah, well, I couldn't argue with that. 'At least you know
for sure now,' I said. 'You got any hard evidence from this
end?'

'No, not yet. My people're still working through his
records, and I told you, he's smart. It won't be just a case
of money left unaccounted for.' He scowled. 'So. What's
the connection with my stepson's murder? You think
there is one?'

'Possibly.' I gave him a rundown of Perilla's theory, that
Paetinius Senior had been behind the killing and
Astrapton had been his son's accomplice in exchange for
the promise of a future bolt-hole.

'That makes sense,' Eutacticus said. His face was set.
'I've lost out to Paetinius over two or three big deals this
last few months. I thought it was just bad luck and
coincidence, but if Astrapton was feeding him inside
information he could've creamed me easy. Which he did.'
He hit the desk again. 'Shit! We're talking millions here,
Corvinus! When I catch the bastard I'll roast him alive!
And as for Paetinius and that son of his –!'

'Uh...it's just a theory, pal,' I said quickly. 'We'll need a lot

116

more proof before we –

But I was talking to myself. Eutacticus was on his feet and heading for the door. He opened it.

'*Critias!*'

'Hold on,' I said. 'What're you doing?'

He ignored me, just waited for the major-domo to put in an appearance. Which he did a few seconds later.

'Yes, sir.'

'Tell Satrius I want to see him.'

'Yes, sir.'

Eutacticus closed the door and went back to the desk.

I had a bad, bad feeling about this. 'Uh...you want to tell me what about?' I said. 'You seeing Satrius, I mean.'

He sat down again. 'I would've thought that was obvious, Corvinus. I told you: nobody messes with my family and gets away with it. The Paetinii are dead meat.'

Shit; he meant it, too. And it was the matter-of-fact tone that sent a chill down my spine. The guy might've been commenting on the weather or the price of grain.

'Hold on,' I said again. 'I told you: it's just a theory, right? No more than that. For all I know it could be complete moonshine, because I've no proof, none. If we can find Astrapton that might be a different matter, but for the moment we're just guessing.'

I got the full ten-candelabra crocodile stare. Then he nodded. 'Okay,' he said. 'You've still got the ball. But if you get the proof then you tell me. Right away. Understood?'

'Yeah. Yeah. Understood.' Jupiter! 'So, uh, how's the search for Astrapton going?'

'Nothing yet, but if he hasn't left Rome then I'll find him. Even if he has, it'll just take a little longer. I've got –'

There was a knock on the door. 'Yes. Come in.'

Satrius. 'You wanted to see me, boss?'

'No. That's all right. I've changed my mind.'

'Only I was coming to see you anyhow. The boys've found Astrapton.'

Eutacticus grinned. 'Have they, indeed? Bring him in.'

'Nah, he isn't here. They just got news of him. Word is, he's holed up in a woman's flat in the Subura.'

'Fine. Go and get him now. Be as rough as you like, but I want him alive and able to talk. Oh, and take Corvinus with you.'

Hey, great. Purple-striper escort duty time again: busy, busy, busy. Still, at least things were moving. And I'd like the chance to have a word with Astrapton myself.

*   *   *

The flat was in one of the better tenements, which seeing

it was the Subura isn't saying much. We weren't alone. Satrius had brought along his sidekick, the one who'd been with him when they'd grabbed me originally and who answered – monosyllabically – to the name of Desmus. It wasn't a talkative journey, but at least we did it on foot and this time around I got through it with my shoulders unmashed.

'Second floor,' Satrius said when we arrived. 'And, Corvinus, you're just along for the ride, okay?'

'Suits me, pal,' I said.

We climbed a staircase with the usual Suburan aroma of soiled nappies, stale urine and faeces. Satrius knocked on the door. No answer. He lifted the latch and pushed. The door opened. I was already getting a bad feeling about this. In the Subura you keep your door locked.

'Wait here,' Satrius said. He went inside. I heard him swear, then he came out again and held the door open for us.

Astrapton was lying on the bed. His throat had been cut, and the knife was in his hand.

'The boss isn't going to be pleased,' Desmus said.

Yeah, well, I reckoned that was an understatement. Still, for a guy with the IQ of a green vegetable prognostication of any kind was a marvel.

I wasn't too happy myself.

Satrius grunted and reached for the knife, but the corpse's fingers were clenched round the hilt. 'Suicide,' he said. 'The bastard got away.'

'You think?' I said.

He gave me a long, slow look while he sucked on a tooth. 'Yeah. That's what I think, smartass,' he said finally. 'Any objections? It's better than he'd get when the boss'd finished with him, and he'd know that. Desmus, search the place.'

That wasn't difficult: apart from a clothes chest and a couple of stools, the bed was the only piece of furniture in the room. There was a bag wedged under it that Astrapton must've brought with him, but like Luscius's that we'd found in the grotto it had nothing more than a spare tunic and a change of underwear.

'That's us done,' Satrius said. 'We might as well go back and report.'

'Hang on, pal,' I said. 'A couple more things. You want to frisk the body?'

That got me another look. Then he shrugged and ran his hands expertly over the corpse. 'Clean,' he said.

'What about the mattress?'

'Fuck off!'

'Just do it. Humour me.'

'Okay. Desmus, take the bastard's ankles. And if I get blood on my tunic, Corvinus, you pay the laundry bill.'

'Sure. Gladly.'

They dumped what was left of Astrapton on the floor and followed him with the mattress. Nothing underneath, just the framework of the bed. Satrius took out his own knife and slit the blood-soaked mattress all the way down one side, then shook out the straw. Nothing.

'Satisfied?' he said.

'Yeah. Yeah, I'm satisfied.'

'Good. Then let's stop fucking around and get back to the Pincian.'

'You go ahead. I'll stay on here for a bit, nose around.'

'You'll come back with us, pal. There's nothing else to see, we don't want to be involved if the Watch get called in, and the boss is going to want to talk to you as well.'

'Have it your way, friend.' We went out, closing the door behind us. 'What about the girl?'

'What girl?' Satrius was already heading down the stairs.

'The girl who rents the flat.'

'She's out at work. Visiting her grandmother. Screwing the High Priest of Jupiter in Cattlemarket Square. How the hell should I know?'

121

'That's not what I meant, pal,' I said. 'What happens when she gets back and finds her boyfriend lying on the floor with his throat slit? How would you feel yourself?'

He grinned. 'I haven't got a boyfriend, Corvinus. What do you want me to do? Clean the place up for her? Now I told you: stop fucking around. The boss'll want to know about this asap.'

Yeah. Right.

One odd thing, though. In fact, it was more than odd. Astrapton'd had time enough to collect a bag with a change of clothes before he split, but on the face of things he hadn't bothered to take any ready cash. Either his own or what he could liberate; he must've had control of some sort of float for necessary business expenses. That just didn't make sense. Whatever he needed if he intended to lie low for a while, cash money in quantity would be pretty high on the list, particularly if his girlfriend wasn't exactly well-heeled, which judging by her choice of accommodation she wasn't. So if the guy had committed suicide and left everything he'd brought to the flat behind him, then where was the bag with the silver? We'd got the Luscius situation again, same pattern, no difference; a missing purse meant that the thing just didn't add up.

Unless, of course, like the Luscius situation it was murder.

TWELVE

'All right,' Eutacticus said when the three of us trooped in *sans* missing accountant. 'What happened? Where the fuck is he?'

'He was dead when we got there, boss,' Satrius said. 'Killed himself.'

Eutacticus looked at me. 'That true, Corvinus?'

'That he was dead, sure,' I said. 'But it wasn't suicide.'

Satrius shot me a glare. 'He had the knife in his hand. What else could it've been?'

Eutacticus was frowning. 'You two. Get out. I'll talk to you later. Corvinus, you sit down.'

I sat. Laughing George and the conversational sprout left, closing the door behind them.

'Now,' Eutacticus said. 'You don't think it was suicide. Care to explain why not?'

'Yeah. There was no purse with the body, and no cash in the guy's pack. Just like your stepson.'

'Maybe he didn't have time to get any money together before he left.'

'He'd time to go to his room and pick up a spare tunic and fresh underwear. Not to mention the pack itself. And he didn't strike me as the sort of guy who wouldn't keep a silver piece or two stashed away for emergencies. Also,

124

what about his office? He have any cash there?'

'Of course he did. That was part of his job, taking care of minor payments. There was a safe built into the desk, with a float of a couple of hundred kept in it, and apart from me he had the only key. He could've taken that easy.' Eutacticus was scowling. 'Hell! You're right, it has to be murder.'

'So who knew? Where he was, I mean?'

'From my side, whoever traced him, obviously. I'll find that out. But I'm telling you now, Corvinus; none of my lads would've killed him. They knew I wanted him alive. And they wouldn't've put off reporting his whereabouts or spreading it around, either, so there's no danger of a leak. When was it done, do you know?'

'Uh-uh. Some time during the morning, obviously, after the girlfriend had left. If your two tame gorillas had been less eager to get back here and bring me with them I might've been able to find something out from the neighbours. I still might, if I try again later.'

'Then you be careful, because the last thing I want is the Watch muscling in on this. As far as they're concerned – as far as anyone's concerned – this was a straightforward suicide, right?'

Oh, bugger. 'Ah...that might be a bit of a moot issue,' I

125

said.

'How so?'

'I, uh, disturbed the scene of the crime a bit.'

'You did *what*?'

I told him about the mattress. 'I needed to be sure he hadn't squirrelled the cash away somewhere in the room, and the bed was the obvious place.'

'Fuck!' He shook his head. 'Well, it's done, and you'd no choice. I'll see what I can do to smooth things over. The girl was nothing special, by all accounts, she can be bought. But you stay clear, Corvinus, and hope nothing comes of it. You hear me?'

Yeah. Well, I supposed that was fair enough, under the circumstances; we'd just have to explore other avenues. I didn't regret it, though; like I'd said, we had to know for sure. 'At least it looks like the accomplice theory is working out,' I said. 'If Astrapton was murdered, which he was, and it wasn't your boys who killed him then it must've been someone on his side of the fence.'

'The Paetinii?'

'Sure. It's a viable hypothesis, anyway, if there was a connection. And making sure he wasn't around to talk would make sense. The only thing that's bugging me is why they would take the money. That wasn't smart, particularly because like I say it points the finger directly at murder where it could conceivably have been suicide.'

'No mystery there. Paetinius is like me, he wouldn't get his own hands dirty, or his son's; he's got people like my Satrius to do his killing for him, and smart is one thing these guys aren't. Not that kind of smart, anyway. Unless they were given strict instructions not to touch it they'd see a purseful of silver pieces as a bonus.'

Yeah, well, given Perilla's theory held good – and I didn't have a better one at present – me, I wasn't so sure the Paetinii weren't involved in person, particularly the son, who hadn't struck me as all that gifted in the forward thinking department: from their point of view, the fewer people who knew of the connection with Astrapton the better. Still, we were on Eutacticus's home ground here; where engineering killings went, he was the expert.

'Right,' I said. 'So the next step is to –'

There was a knock on the door and a little dapper guy came in clutching an armful of writing tablets. I recognised him as the clerk from the office next to Astrapton's who'd told Sempronia and me that Astrapton was in a meeting with the boss.

'Yes, Lucius, what is it?' Eutacticus said.

'We've found some definite anomalies, sir.' The guy laid

the tablets on the desk. 'Quite a few of them, I'm afraid.
The total here comes to something just under two
million.'

Eutacticus stared at him. 'Two fucking *million?*'

'Spread over the past eighteen months. And we haven't
finished checking yet. There may be a good deal more.
He was clever, sir. Double entries, false payments that
don't work out, inflated outgoings, that sort of thing. A
steady, constant drain. But you'd never know unless you
looked. I mean, *really* looked.'

'Shit!' Eutacticus's fist hit the desk, dislodging the pile.
Writing tablets slid to the floor. 'So where's the money?'

'I don't know, sir. There'd be far too much to hide, even in
gold, and we've had his office and his room torn apart.
Literally, sir, floorboards, ceiling panels, everything.
There's nothing, nothing at all.'

'I want it fucking found!'

'We're trying, sir. We think he must've set up some sort
of transfer arrangement. A private account with a banker,
probably using another name –'

'The hell with that! We're talking millions here! There isn't
an honest banker in the city who wouldn't know there
was something screwy about a freedman with no
identifiable business connections making regular

deposits on that scale, and start asking questions. And any dishonest one who knew what he'd be getting into wouldn't touch the bastard with a bargepole, because he'd also know that when I found out – which I would, eventually – I'd be down on him like a ton of fucking bricks.'

'There is one thing, sir.' The guy reached down nervously and picked up one of the fallen tablets. 'It's a very recent entry, made only yesterday, in fact. On the face of it, it's quite innocuous, but...well, judge for yourself.' He opened the tablet and handed it over. 'The one on the fifth line.'

Eutacticus took the tablet and scanned the entries.

'"One crate marble statues to Larus",' he said. 'So?'

'We've looked, sir. We can find no record of a corresponding order from anyone by that name. As a customer, he just doesn't exist. The point is, there are entries for single crates going to the same person at roughly two-monthly intervals over the past eight months. That's four in all, including the latest one. Not always statues, sir, but always a crate. And none of the entries tie in with any order received. As I say, it could be nothing, but –'

'So who is this Larus?'

'We don't know, sir. At least, like I said, he's not in our

records as a customer. But I did ask a friend in the...in one of your other departments, the one concerned with the more, ah, clandestine side of the business.' He glanced sideways at me, but I was playing selectively blind and deaf.

'And?' Eutacticus said.

'There is a small-time operator by that name. Publius Publilius. Larus is his nickname, "Seagull". I can give you his address, if you want it.'

'You've done well, Lucius.' Eutacticus turned to me. 'What d'you think, Corvinus? Worth checking?'

'Sure,' I said. 'Lucius, where can I find this guy?'

'He has a bric-a-brac shop south of the Circus, sir. Near the Temple of Aesculapius.'

'Fine.' I got up. 'Right, I can see you two have matters of business to discuss. I'll get in touch, Eutacticus, if I've any news.'

'You don't want Satrius or one of the lads to go with you?'

'No. Not this time. And me, I'd keep this quiet for the time being. We've already lost one lead. If this Publilius is involved then we don't want him to go the same way if we can avoid it.'

'You think there could've been a leak on our side after all?'

I shrugged. 'I'm not taking any chances. But if I find the guy has unfortunately and coincidentally decided to slit his own throat in the interim as well, then I'll know where to start asking questions. Right, Lucius?'

The little clerk swallowed. 'Sir, I wouldn't!' he said. 'Honestly!'

'See that you don't, then,' I said, and left.

*　*　*

It was too late in the day now for the long hike down to Circus Valley; besides, I reckoned we'd done pretty well. Publilius could wait for tomorrow.

THIRTEEN

Bric-a-brac was dignifying things. What Publilius sold was junk, or the next thing to it: iron bedframes with half their struts missing, cooking pots that were more patches than original metal, third-hand tunics, and a selection of miscellaneous items such as bronze letters for (or possibly prised from) inscriptions. Not, I knew, that what was on sale would be the mainstay of the business. That'd be the middleman service shopkeepers like Publilius provided linking the gentlemen who made sure certain items fell off the back of a delivery cart and the said items' eventual end-users.

I was examining a worm-eaten wooden leg that I'd seen leaning against a brazier with its grate burned out when the man himself oiled over.

'Morning, sir,' he said. 'Anything I can do for you?'

'Sure.' I put the leg down where I'd found it. 'Marble statues.'

'Buying or selling?'

'Just expressing an interest at present, pal,' I said. 'You deal in them?'

'I might do.' He was cautious. 'That depends. Say you give me a such-as?'

'Okay. Such as a crateful. Sent to you in the past couple

of days by someone called Gaius Astrapton. Plus three other crates, contents miscellaneous, sender ditto. Ring any bells?'

He looked blank, then angry. 'Who the hell are you?' he said. 'And what's this about?'

'Just answer the question, friend.'

'Then the answer's no. I don't know nothing about no crate of statues. Nor any other crates. And I don't know no Gaius Astrapton, neither. Now push off. I've got a business to run.'

I was puzzled; there hadn't been a glimmer there, not a glint. If he was lying then he was damn good at it. Or he'd been warned I was coming.

'How about Sempronius Eutacticus?' I said. 'You heard of him?'

He blinked. 'Yeah. I've heard of Eutacticus. So?'

'He was the one gave me your name and asked me to drop round and see you,' I said. 'Astrapton was his accountant. Seemingly, he's been going into business off his own bat, and Eutacticus is really, really keen to know the details. According to his records, he's sent you four crates in all in the last eight months. Now stop fucking around, pal.'

Publilius scowled. 'I told you,' he said. 'I don't know

nothing about no statues, nor crates neither. You don't believe me, you can look for yourself.'

'I'll just do that, if you don't mind.'

I went into the shop. It was bigger than I thought it would be: he'd knocked through the wall of the private building behind it and taken over one of the rooms. The rear section was separated off from the front by a curtain, which I pushed aside and went through. Publilius followed.

'Look all you like,' he said.

There was plenty of stuff, sure, piled up wall to wall. Better stuff than he'd got on show outside, too: bales of cloth, furniture with all the bits attached, a wide selection of ornaments and a complete Corinthian dinner service. There was even a water-clock. Still, nothing that looked like it'd make a hole in two million sesterces, let alone the pile of cash itself filling a sizeable chest in the form of gold bricks. Because, with that amount of loot involved, that's what it would mean. And no intact crates, singular or plural.

'Satisfied?' he said.

'No.'

'Then that's your hard luck. What you see is what you get.'

I grabbed him by the neck of his tunic. He froze.

'Listen carefully, pal,' I said, 'because I'm only going to say this once. Eutacticus is out two million sesterces through your friend Astrapton, and he is consequently not a happy bunny. Me, I couldn't care less about the money, or about Eutacticus for that matter, and I'm the good guy. Talk to me now and I'll say you co-operated right down the line, that you thought the whole thing was legit. Keep your mouth zipped and the next person to ask won't do it so politely. In fact, considering that the next person will be a large and very unpleasant gentleman by the name of Satrius, politeness in any form will be right off the agenda. Understand?'

I let him go. He was breathing heavily as he straightened his tunic.

'Now you listen,' he said. 'I'm a small-time fence, right? Admitted, no argument, everyone's got to live. You bring me a set of snail-spoons or a silver wine jug or even a fucking dinner table and I'll pay you top rate without asking no questions. If you're buying then I'll cut you a good deal so long as you don't ask for no bill of sale. But that's as far as I go. I've heard of Eutacticus, sure, who hasn't? But I don't know no Astrapton, and I don't know nothing about no fucking mystery crates. If Eutacticus himself wants to come and ask me I'll tell him the same thing. So get off my back, right?'

Hell. As far as sounding convincing went, you didn't get much better. Maybe we'd been mistaken after all. Avenue closed. So what did I do now?

The answer to that was easy. When all else fails, rattle some bars and see what jumps.

It was time to have a word with Paetinius. Not the son; the father.

FOURTEEN

If you made the usual allowances for artistic licence and flattery, the elder Patinius was a dead ringer for his portrait in the atrium: little, tubby, and smug. That is, until you looked at his eyes, which were ice-grey chips of marble.

'I won't pretend I don't know why you're here and who you represent, Corvinus,' he said, putting his hands on the desk – we were in the study – and lacing the fingers together. 'Or that you're welcome in my house. Sestia told me all about your last visit. She also said that she practically threw you out. Can you give me a reason why I shouldn't do the same?'

I gave him my best smile. 'Yes, I can, pal,' I said. 'It's because you're curious.'

'Curious about what?'

'What I know and don't know. How far I've got. How safe you are. That sort of thing. Me, I'd like to know that too, because at the end of the day I think you're in this up to your neck. So look on this as a trade.'

The eyes rested on me for a moment. Then he grunted and got up.

'Come with me,' he said.

He led me through to the atrium and up to the family

shrine in the corner. There was a pan of incense smoking on it, in front of the little images of the household gods. He pointed to it.

'Know what that's for?' he said.

I shrugged. 'No. Anything special?'

'It's a thank-you offering. For that bastard Eutacticus's son and heir being dead. Potential son and heir.' He reached over to the bowl of raw incense on the small table next to the shrine and added another pinch to the smoking pan. 'That answer your question?'

'You're admitting it? That you had Titus Luscius killed?'

'I'm admitting or denying nothing. Why should I make your job easier? Maybe I did, maybe I didn't. But if I did, I've no regrets. No fears, either, because I've got people of my own, and if Publius Eutacticus wants to start something I can give as good as I can get. On the other hand, if I didn't then whoever did has my blessing. That clear enough for you?'

'Yeah. Clear, sure, but not particularly illuminating.'

'Fine. Like I said, that's your problem, not mine. So let's go back into the study where we can talk in comfort until I decide to throw you out.'

We did. Paetinius settled into his chair behind the desk. 'Okay,' he said. 'I'm all ears. Make your pitch.'

I sat down opposite him. 'You had a deal going with Eutacticus's accountant Astrapton, who was ripping off his employer. You paid off his gambling debt at the Golden Fleece and promised him a bolt-hole if things got difficult. In exchange, he supplied inside information on Eutacticus's upcoming business deals and acted as facilitator and accomplice in your plans for getting rid of his stepson. You wanted Luscius out of the way because Eutacticus was planning to adopt him formally. Which would mean your own son – who might well be Eutacticus's – would be out of the legal running if Eutacticus died without a clear male heir.'

I paused for comment, but Paetinius didn't respond, or even give an indication that he'd noticed. His face didn't give anything away, either.

'Astrapton set Luscius up; how he managed that I'm not exactly sure yet, but the details don't matter. In any case, he decoyed him and his slave to the grotto at the back of the garden. Your son had come over the wall earlier – or it may not've been your son, just one of your "people", again it doesn't matter – and together they did the actual killing. Then they hid the bodies in the grotto, Astrapton pretended he'd seen the two of them leave, and that was that.' I stopped again, and waited. Nothing. The guy's face was still expressionless, and again he hadn't moved. I could've been talking to myself. 'You care to comment, pal?'

Paetinius grunted and shrugged. 'It's an interesting theory, I'll give you that much,' he said.

'And?'

'Where it falls down is that most of it's a load of balls.'

'Really? You care to tell me which bits aren't, maybe?'

'Certainly. I bought Astrapton, sure, you have that right, and he was cheap at the price. Best twenty-five thousand I ever spent, and would've been even if I hadn't had a copper of it back just to know I was rubbing Eutacticus's nose in the shit. As it is, from what I made out of information supplied I reckon I'm a good two or three million up on the deal, so I'm not complaining, especially if Eutacticus knows now that I've been responsible for shafting him. Same goes for giving Astrapton a new place. I can always use a smart young man with a good working knowledge of the business, and if he's decided that it's time for a career change then I'd be delighted to oblige.' He smiled, but the marble-chip eyes didn't change. 'Particularly since it'll mean pushing that bastard on the Pincian's face just a little bit deeper down.'

'Yeah, well, there's a slight problem with that now, isn't

there?'

The smile disappeared. 'How do you mean?'

'Astrapton's dead. Someone cut his throat for him.'

'*What?*'

'Don't tell me. You didn't know.'

'Of course I didn't. Why should I?'

'If my theory's right after all, pal, you'd have reason. The guy was an embarrassing loose end connecting you with young Luscius's murder. Besides, he'd already served his purpose. His cover was blown, and if he'd cheated on one boss he could cheat on another. All in all, he'd be better off out of the way.'

'You're saying I killed him?'

'It'd make sense. You or your son or your people, the details don't matter. And you'd know where he was holed up, because if he was planning on that career change he'd've made sure you knew how to get in touch.'

Paetinius laughed. 'Corvinus, that's pure garbage. I'd no idea where Astrapton was, I'd nothing to do with his death, and as sure as hell I wasn't responsible for Luscius's.' He stood up. 'Now piss off. Interview over.'

Well, I'd hardly been expecting him to come up with an admission. And if he was guilty – the jury was still well and truly out on that one – then I reckoned that as far as bars-rattling went I'd done a pretty good job. I got up, thanked him politely for his time, and pissed off.

*　　*　　*

The sun was into its third quarter when I came down Patricius Incline to the main drag. There was no point in rushing straight home, and besides a bit of quiet contemplation and retrenching was in order. Not to mention a light lunch: I'd skipped breakfast, and after walking across half of Rome my tongue was hanging out. So I found a little wineshop tucked away in a courtyard off Staurus Street and settled in with a half-jug of Praetutian, some Picenan bread and a plateful of goat's cheese and olives.

Right; so what had we got? More exactly, what hadn't we got? Bars-rattling was all very well, but the Larus angle hadn't proved too promising, to say the least. Publilius had been a crook, sure, but he was small-time and by his lights he'd struck me as honest enough; if we were looking for a destination for Astraptus's crates then I'd bet a fairly hefty sum that he wasn't it. He had too much to lose for a start; like Eutacticus had said, anyone who was on the shady side of things wouldn't touch Astrapton with a bargepole, because they'd know that however big and tempting their cut of the deal was when Eutacticus found out they'd be swimming the Tiber with concrete sandals. My guess was that this Larus was an innocent who didn't know what he was into, a shipper or a carter that Astrapton had contracted to transfer the goodies to a safe location, probably using a false name as well as the false description of the crates' contents. In which case the chances of finding him were practically zilch: Rome and Ostia are full of small entrepreneurs who'll gladly take on orders where not much actual bulk's involved, and who wouldn't ask too many questions so long as they get their money upfront, because why should they? All this assuming, of course, that Larus was a real name and not one that Astrapton had used for his own reference, avoiding the actual one for reasons of security and maybe even choosing it deliberately to point anyone snooping in the wrong direction, so that even 'practically zilch' was an optimistic assessment...

Bugger. The more I thought about it the worse it got. Paetinius, though, was another matter. That guy I wouldn't've trusted as far as I could spit, because as far as helping Astrapton to squirrel away his ill-gotten gains was concerned he had motive, means and opportunity in spades. For a start, he hated Eutacticus like poison, and making things easy for his accountant to smuggle a couple of million sesterces'-worth of bullion out from under his nose would've tickled his questionable sense of humour no end. Second, who else would Astrapton turn to? He's working for the guy already, so he's the natural choice; and if Paetinius didn't object to his protégé doing a bit of moonlighting – which I'd bet he wouldn't – he couldn't do any better, because Paetinius would have the contacts to make the thing happen. And it would be yet another reason, besides the security aspect of things, for Paetinius to stiff him: if he knew what Astrapton had done with the money, then once the guy was safely dead he could collect himself and be another two million up on the deal.

For much the same reasons I didn't put too much credence into his denial of involvement in Luscius's death, either: for him and his son to be responsible fitted both the facts and the theory like a glove. And that he wouldn't've admitted to, never, no way, nohow. Screwing a competitor financially is one thing; however much Eutacticus foamed at the mouth and cursed the guy blue, he'd accepted that it'd been just in the way of business, or whatever you like to call it. But murdering one of the guy's family was a whole different ball game. I'd heard Eutacticus on the subject, and if I'd gone back to him to report that Paetinius had admitted having Luscius killed it would've been war to the knife. Paetinius wouldn't risk that, no matter how confident he was that he could look after himself.

So Paetinius – or rather the Paetinii, father and son – were still firmly in the frame, and currently the only game in town. What I needed, though, was proof, and that was the bugger because I hadn't the least idea how to get it. Ah, well. No doubt things would work out in the end. And Perilla might have some thoughts on the subject.

I finished off the wine and nibbles – not too impressive, either of them; I wouldn't be revisiting this place – and headed back to the Caelian.

FIFTEEN

When I got home, the lady was pacing the atrium and fizzing. In her best togs, too.

'Marcus, where have you been?' she snapped.

'Uh...'

'You've forgotten, haven't you?'

'Forgotten what?'

'Dinner with Lippillus and Marcina, of course.'

Oh, hell. She'd got me bang to rights. It'd been arranged a month ago, Meton squared and everything. We didn't go out much, but dinner with my Watch pal Decimus Lippillus and his wife, either at their place or ours, was a regular event. And this time it was at their place on the Aventine, which made matters worse because we'd have to get there.

'Look, I'm sorry, lady,' I said. 'Things intervened.'

'Well, you're here now. You've no time for a bath, just a quick wash and brush up. I've told Bathyllus to lay out a clean party mantle, and the litter's ready and waiting. We can still make it if you hurry.'

'What about Agron and Cass?' My other long-term pal, the big Illyrian and his Alexandrian-Greek wife Cassiopeia, who'd been invited as well. Like they always did when they came up to Rome, they'd be staying over with us.

'They arrived hours ago and went on ahead. Now *move!*'

I moved.

*   *   *

We made it with nothing to spare, the litter-slaves pulling up outside Lippillus's tenement, nostrils flaring and sweating like thoroughbreds. Not that I had much sympathy for the bastards: they weren't exactly overworked, and all of them could use a couple of inches off the waistline.

The tenement was new, built for the upper end of the market, and Lippillus had only just moved in, so this was the first time I'd seen the place. He'd done a deal with the owner for a long lease on two first-floor apartments, and used his Watch Commander contacts with the city's Department of Buildings and Public Works to convert them into a single flat with more going for it than you usually find, even in first-floor top-of-the-range properties. No internal plumbing, of course, but at least from what the guy had told me there was more than enough room to swing a cat, which was rare in any tenement block, and the architect had even managed a small kitchen. Considering that there were no kids to complicate matters – unlike the situation at Agron and Cass's place in Ostia, where they were five up and counting – he and Marcina were pretty well set up.

We climbed the stairs. Lippillus must've been watching from the window, because the front door was open and he was waiting for us.

'Hey, Marcus, how's the boy?' he said.

'Not bad.' I handed him the jar of Setinian I'd brought with me. 'Housewarming present.'

He beamed: Lippillus was almost as fond of a good wine as I was, but Watch Commanders' pay doesn't stretch to jars of the top-grade stuff. 'You mind if we don't open it now? Only Agron's brought along a jar he and Cass got from one of his brothers-in-law, and I've got some of that ready mixed. From a vineyard near Massilia.'

'No problem, pal.' I'd mental reservations, sure – Agron's thing was cheese, not wine, and neither he nor Cass were serious wine drinkers – but a guest doesn't dictate what booze his host serves. Besides, I'm always up to try something new, and Gallic wines in general were coming along nicely, as long as they travelled.

'And these are for Marcina.' Perilla, a step or two behind me, had been carrying a tray of custard pastries with glazed fruit and nuts on top. 'Meton made them specially, from a Syrian recipe he's been meaning to try.' Marcina, like Cass, had a sweet tooth, although unlike in Cass's case the consequences didn't show: Marcina Paullina could still've modelled for Praxiteles's Athena, easy. Not just round the waist, either.

'Great!' Lippillus kissed her on both cheeks. 'We can have them for dessert. You could use Marcina's pastries for doorstops. Come on in.'

We did. The living-cum-dining-room wasn't big, but this was a tenement flat after all, and with what had been a couple of the original partition walls taken away there was more than enough floor space for the usual three couches and central table. Agron and Cass were stretched out on one of the couches with wine cups in front of them, and the starters were already in place.

'Hi, Corvinus,' Agron said. 'You made it, then?'

'On two wheels. Eight feet, rather. My fault entirely.'

'Marcina's in the kitchen putting the final touches to the main course,' Lippillus said. 'You want to take that tray straight through to her, Perilla? We're just about ready to eat.'

'Yeah. I'm sorry about that, pal.' I lay down on the other side couch. 'Something came up.'

'A case?' Lippillus was ladling wine from the mixing bowl on another table to the side into a third cup. He handed it to me. 'Here. See what you think.'

I sipped. Not bad; not bad at all. Not quite Alban standard, but close. Very close. 'I'm impressed.'

Agron grinned. 'Cass's brother Timon had it as a gift from a customer,' he said. 'The guy deals in kitchenware, mostly, but he knows his wines and he owns a small vineyard just north of Massilia. Not a commercial setup, just for his own use, so he can afford to concentrate on quality. Surrentine vines, yoke trussing, low yield. We did a deal over a repair job.'

Yeah, that made sense: what with Ostia's shipping trade in decline, Agron's carpentry business mostly dealt in carts these days, but Cass's family had been involved with ship-building and ships in general for generations and ship repairs were still an occasional sideline. Particularly where family was concerned. Timon, I knew, like most of Cass's considerable number of male siblings and cousins in both Ostia and Alexandria, was in the shipping trade itself, and deals in that direction tended to be in kind and/or favours owed rather than cash.

Lippillus filled a cup for himself and lay down on the top couch. 'So,' he said. 'What's the case?'

I gave him the basic rundown. He frowned when I mentioned Eutacticus – organised crime bosses aren't exactly flavour of the month with Watch Commanders, particularly when they double as clients – but he didn't comment. 'That's about as far as I've got at present,' I finished. 'The Paetinii are in it up to their eyeballs, that I'd swear to, but proving it's another matter.'

'It adds up, certainly. I don't know anything about the son, barring that he's in with a pretty fast set socially, but Paetinius Senior's no wide-eyed innocent, that's for sure.' Lippillus chewed on a stuffed olive. 'And he may not be quite in Sempronius Eutacticus's league yet, but he's getting there fast. If you do manage to nail him, Marcus, I'd be very interested. And, of course, anything I can do to help just let me know.'

'There is something,' I said. 'It may not be important, because as far as I know it has nothing directly to do either with the Paetinii or with young Luscius's death, but it's the only lead I've got at present and I may as well chase it. The dead accountant. Astrapton. He left a record of a contact he was using to squirrel away the bullion he'd been creaming off the top of Eutacticus's profits. Or at least I think that's how it worked, assuming it isn't a false trail. Name of Larus. Ring any bells?'

'"Seagull"? No, not offhand, although I can ask around. Leave it with me.'

'You're sure he's a person, Corvinus?' Agron said.

'What?'

'Only Seagull's a common name for a boat.'

Everything went very still. 'Is that so, now?' I said.

'Yeah. In Ostia, anyway.'

Oh, gods! 'You happen to know of any in particular?'

'Sure. A good dozen, at least.'

Bugger. Still, it was a start, and I felt the first prickle of excitement. 'Could you make me a list?'

'Hold on. It's not that bad. You're talking merchantmen, right? Not small fishing boats?' I nodded; for this to work it would have to be a merchantman, big enough to carry crates, at least. 'Going where?'

I shrugged. 'Pass. Does it matter?'

'It would narrow the field. Most have their own routes, and they tend to stick to them. South along the coast or across to Gaul and Spain are the usual ones. To the south as far as Sicily, maybe even Mauretania and Africa, although barring grain barges most of the real long-distance ships work out of Puteoli. If you don't have a destination I can think of two possibles. For Ostia, at least.'

'Three,' Cass said.

Hey, great! Three I could live with. 'Namely?'

'Titus Secundus, for one. He works the Tyrrhenian circuit. Corsica, Sardinia, down to Lilybaeum and Panormus then back home via Naples. Then there's Gaius Imber. He's Massilia/New Carthage, like Timon.' He turned to Cass. 'Who's your third, love?'

'Gaius Florus.'

Agron nodded. 'Old Florus. Right. I'd forgotten him. He's practically retired. He used to work the Sicily route until he lost his son in a storm off Cape Peloris, but he does mostly inshore work on the northern side now, up as far as Genua.'

Yeah, well; all three sounded fair bets. Certainly Genua, Sicily and the coasts of Gaul and Spain would all be far enough away from Rome and Eutacticus to provide Astrapton with a reasonably secure bolt-hole for whenever he wanted to use it, particularly since getting his loot to any one of them need only have been the first step to disappearing into the tall timber. That was always assuming I wasn't chasing moonbeams here to begin with, naturally, or that as far as Titus Luscius's murder was concerned finding Larus – *the* Larus – wasn't irrelevant. But you have to make certain assumptions, and like I said as leads went it was the only game in town at present. I couldn't afford to be picky, and I've always believed in the maxim that if you keep digging then sooner or later you're bound to turn something up. Besides, I'd got an itch at the back of my neck, and that'd always been a good sign.

'So how would I find these guys?' I said. 'They in port currently?'

'That I don't know. I can find out, sure, and if they are I can talk to them myself, but it'd take time, I wouldn't know what questions to ask, and I'd have to get back to you. It's likely enough, though, because there's less than a month of the sailing season still to run, so if any of the three of them haven't actually made their last round trip of the year already they'll be on the inward leg. But if you're really interested then the best plan would be to come down to Ostia yourself and stay on until you've got what you need.'

'We can put you up,' Cass said. 'It'd be no trouble.'

'Ah –'

Agron grinned. 'Not at the flat, Corvinus. I wouldn't do that to you. The family upstairs from us has just moved to Capua, and we haven't found replacements yet. You could use that, and welcome. It's no palace, but it's clean and furnished.'

I breathed a mental sigh of relief. Bunking down in a

tenement I didn't mind, particularly in the short term – I'd done it before, years back, in Aelius Sejanus's time, and for a lot longer than a few days – but just the thought of sharing a flat *sine die* with five screaming kids brought me out in a cold sweat. I wouldn't be exactly slumming it, either: Cass, as the tenement's live-in owner, had pretty exacting standards where conditions and the choice of tenants were concerned. The outgoing family would've been vetted from the start six ways from nothing, and if they'd been allowed to leave the place in anything but pristine condition I'd eat my sandals.

'Fine, pal,' I said. 'I might well just take you up on that.'

...which was when Marcina and Perilla came back in from their mini kitchen klatch, and I had to drop the subject for the duration. Don't ask me why, because it makes no sense, but the lady has a deep-seated aversion to talking murder at dinner parties, and if she'd caught me at it there would've been hell to pay later. Lippillus would've got it in the neck, too, from Marcina, for allowing it.

Still, things were moving again. Or at least I hoped they were.

SIXTEEN

We'd just settled down to breakfast on the terrace the next morning – Agron and Cass were staying over for another couple of days – when Bathyllus buttled in to say I had a visitor.

Oh, shit: Laughing George again. Didn't that guy work regular hours like everyone else? 'Okay, little guy,' I said wearily. 'Show him through.'

But it wasn't Satrius this time. It was Sempronia's maid. She was looking more scrunched-up than ever: a little mouse of a girl who radiated apology for existing. She followed Bathyllus through the folding doors like she was going to her own execution and stood beside the table, eyes lowered and silent.

'Uh…Cleo, isn't it?' I said.

'Cleia, sir.' I hadn't heard her speak before, and her voice was as quiet and mousey as the rest of her.

'Right. Sorry.' Perilla was looking at me with amusement. Agron and Cass were just looking. 'So what can I do for you?'

'It's difficult, sir. If I could just talk to you in private?'

'Sure. No problem.' I got up. 'We'll go inside.'

I took her arm – she was shivering – , led her into the atrium and plonked her down on the nearest couch.

'Now,' I said. 'What is it? A message from your mistress?'

'No, sir. At least, she did send me, but it's something I had to tell you myself.'

'Go ahead.'

She took a deep breath. 'It's about Satrius, sir.'

Which was as far as she got before clamming up again. Jupiter! This was like pulling teeth! And I'm never at my best with terrified, mousey little slave girls. 'You want to talk to Perilla rather than me, Cleia?' I said. 'I can get her if –'

'*No!*' The eyes came up; they were red-rimmed, with black shadows under them. 'The mistress said it had to be you. You'd know what to do.'

'Okay.' I sat down beside her. 'In your own time, then. But I don't bite.'

'He killed Astrapton.'

'*What?*'

'It's true, sir. Or at least I think it is.'

'Ah…you care to tell me why?' I had to fight to keep my voice level.

'He knew where he was hiding.'

'Yeah. Yeah, of course he did. I went round with him myself, and –'

'No. Before. Three days ago.'

157

I sat back. '*Three* days ago? But –' This didn't make sense. I'd been there in Eutacticus's study when Satrius had told him that Astrapton had just been traced. And that was two days ago, not three, after we'd got back from the Golden Fleece. Satrius hadn't known where Astrapton was then…

Or at least if he had he'd kept the information to himself. Shit!

'How do you know?' I said calmly.

'My brother told me.'

'Your *brother?*'

'My brother Alexander, sir. He said he told Satrius where to look for Astrapton – where to start looking, at least – the day before he died.'

My brain was whirling. 'That was pretty fast work,' I said. 'The word didn't go out that Astrapton had done a runner until three days ago. So how did your brother know where he'd gone?'

'He's one of the clerks, sir. They got on together, him and Astrapton. They shared the same interests.' She glanced up at me quickly under lowered lashes. 'Girls. That sort of thing. You know? About a month ago, Astrapton mentioned one he'd found one in the Subura who worked as a dancer in a club called Cupid's Bow.'

'You have a name, maybe? For the girl, I mean.'

'Lysidice. At least, I think that was it. He'd set her up in a flat of her own, in the tenement next door. Astrapton could afford that. He always had plenty of money.'

'Okay. Go on.'

'Alexander's clever, sir. When Astrapton disappeared, he –'

'Put two and two together. Right.' Gods! 'And he told Satrius all this, yes?'

'As soon as he knew Astrapton was missing.'

Three days ago. Sure, it fitted: with a definite address in his pocket, Laughing George could've gone straight to the poor bastard and zeroed him before he had time to unpack. The only question – and it was the biggie – was why?

Unless he was working for Paetinius Senior, of course. And that opened a whole new can of worms.

Mind you, if that was the case then the guy was running a hell of a risk. If Eutacticus found out – which, now, he would, because I'd tell him myself assuming the girl's story checked out; I couldn't risk not doing it – then Satrius was crows'-meat. 'Can I talk to your brother directly?'

She looked frightened. *'No! Please!'*

'Why not?'

'He saw me leaving the house. Satrius, I mean. This morning.'

'So?'

'He knows that Alexander knows. He knows he's my brother. If he suspected anything, if he followed me, then –!' Forget frightened; the kid was terrified. 'Sir, I wouldn't've come at all if the mistress hadn't sent me! She made me come! *Please!*'

I stood up. 'Look,' I said. 'Your brother's in no danger, right? Satrius isn't a fool. If he hasn't tried anything yet – which he hasn't – then he wouldn't dare do it now, not with me and your mistress both knowing the story. If the guy came to any harm as far as he's concerned it'd only put the lid on things.' Shit; Perilla'd be a lot better at this than I would. Reassurance wasn't my bag. Where was the lady when I needed her? 'Okay. Compromise. You get back. If Satrius should ask you where you've been, or even if he has followed you and knows you came here, you tell him that your mistress sent you to ask me whether I have any more news. The answer was no. Tell Sempronia from me she'll have to confirm that if need be. You got that?'

She nodded dumbly.

'Good. I'll drop by later today and –'

'*No!*'

'Cleia, listen. It's no big deal. I've been to the house twice before, and I was meaning to come round today in any case. Talk it over with Sempronia and your brother. If he does decide to see me personally –' She shivered and clutched herself. '*If* he does, then we can work something out. In that case there'll be no risk, none, I guarantee it. Now off you go. And thank you.'

She left, and I sat back down on the couch to think.

Okay. It made some kind of sense, and it fitted in with the theory so far. Where Astrapton's death was concerned, it cleared up the problem of timing: Eutacticus's organisation might've been efficient, but a scant two days between the guy walking out of the gate and being traced to a Suburan flat was pretty good going. I should've wondered about that at the time. Oh, sure, the theory held good where the actual murder was concerned: if Astrapton was working for Paetinius, which he was by the guy's own admission, then it was well within the bounds of credibility that Paetinius would know where to find him, and if he was killed on Paetinius's orders that part of things was cut and dried. But Eutacticus's team was another matter. Without any firm leads to go on – and if there had been I'd never known what they were – it should've taken a lot longer than it did. The Subura's a big place, and Rome itself's a hell of a lot bigger.

It fitted in with the circumstances of young Luscius's death, too. *Pace* what I'd said to Perilla, I'd never been quite happy with the explanation there: from what I'd seen of them both, neither of our two theoretical murderers quite came up to scratch: I didn't know how the slave Lynchus weighed in, but Titus Luscius's friend Bellarius had said the guy was no pushover where fighting went. You'd have to factor in the element of surprise, sure, and that might well be crucial, but neither Astrapton nor Paetinius were expert killers. Satrius was, in spades; if need be, I'd bet that he could've taken both Luscius and his slave easily. And if both he and Astrapton were working for the same boss then it was a partnership made in heaven. Or wherever.

It explained other things, too: Satrius's reluctance, when we found Astrapton's body, to let me talk to his girlfriend's neighbours, and the missing cash; Eutacticus himself had said that it'd be second nature to any of his hit-men, or Paetinius's, to liberate any pouches they found lying around.

Yeah. It added up. What precisely it added up *to*, I didn't fully understand yet. But at least for once we were ahead of the game. So long as Satrius didn't know he'd been rumbled. I just hoped, whatever assurances I'd given Cleia, that he didn't.

Meanwhile, I'd got a name and a place: Lysidice, and the Cupid's Bow club, next door to where we'd found the body. Even if I didn't get to speak to Alexander, I could do a bit of independent checking. If it got me involved with the local Watch re Astrapton's death, then tough: I'd just have to get Lippillus to put in a good word for me with his opposite number in the Fourth District. And if Eutacticus had any complaints he could go and screw himself.

*   *   *

Luckily Agron had arranged to see a man about a big cart-building contract that morning, and Cass had gone off with Perilla on one of their usual shop-until-you-drop binges where male company is positively discouraged, so I was free of the usual host obligations for the present. I walked over to the Subura and found the street where Satrius had taken me three days before. Sure enough, next to the tenement Astrapton had died in was a two-storey building with a plaque set into the wall beside the door showing Cupid taking aim at a lady wearing a smirk and not much else. At that range, and given the breadth of the target, the kid couldn't miss. The door was locked, which was par for the course at this time of day. I knocked and kept on knocking until the grille opened.

'Piss off,' the guy behind it said. 'We're closed until sunset.'

The reaction wasn't exactly unexpected. I didn't have Laughing George with me this time, but I did have the magic words.

'You want me to go back and tell Sempronius Eutacticus that?' I said.

The door was opened with alacrity.

'I'm sorry, sir,' the slave said. 'What can I do for you?'

'The boss in?'

'Yes, sir. Just go straight through.'

I did, into the main room of the club itself. Forget the Fleece; Cupid's Bow was pretty basic, with nothing but a low stage, a bar area, some third-class murals on the wall that looked like they'd been painted by a particularly dirty-minded but talentless child of six, and a few unmatched tables and chairs that any self-respecting auction room in Rome would've sold off for scrap. This was the Subura, after all, and what the local punters were interested in was naked flesh and booze at rock-bottom prices, not flashy décor.

The owner – that had to be him, sitting at one of the tables, tucking into a late breakfast or early lunch of bread and bean stew – fitted the place. Sleazy, greasy and with as much visible appeal as a snot-filled handkerchief.

'Yeah?' he said through a mouthful of the local cookshop's best. 'What's your business?'

'The name's Marcus Corvinus, pal,' I said. 'I'm representing Sempronius Eutacticus.'

The magic words again. He swallowed, stood up and brushed crumbs and stray beans off his tunic. I could grow to like this.

'Eutacticus?'

'That's right. He understands you've got a girl working here. A dancer. Name of Lysidice.'

'What does Eutacticus want with her?'

'Just a five-minute chat. Or rather, I do as his rep. She does work here, then?'

'Did. I haven't seen her for days. Not since her boyfriend was found stiff in her room with his throat cut. She's cleared out completely.' He belched. 'That what this is about?'

'More or less. The boyfriend was Eutacticus's

accountant.'

'Oh, fuck!' The guy swallowed again. Not beans this time; he just swallowed. 'He thinks she did it?'

'No. He knows who was responsible. He's just curious about the details. Hence the visit.'

'Me, I don't know nothing.'

It could be true, of course. If I'd been the Watch, sure, it would've been the instinctive reply from any Suburan worth his salt, the verbal equivalent of a knee-jerk, and I'd've discounted it as such on principle. On the other hand, when one of Eutacticus's reps – self-styled, naturally, but he wasn't to know that – was the person doing the asking it was more believable. Not completely believable, mind, but there you went. A little pressure might do it.

'Come on, pal,' I said. 'You can do better than that, surely? The boss really, *really* wants hard information here. If I ask around, maybe the girl's neighbours, and find you were holding out on me then when I tell him he isn't going to be very pleased, is he?'

The guy practically whimpered. 'Okay,' he said. 'She was back in here not long after she'd finished her stint and gone home, in a bit of a state, saying she was in trouble and asking for money.'

'This was the night before? Before the body was discovered, I mean?'

'That's right.'

'You give her it? The money?'

'Lysidice's a nice girl. Never any trouble, like most of them are, never asked for a sub before. And she was desperate, I could see that. I paid her the wages she was owed, maybe a touch more.'

Okay; so that fixed the time of the murder to the previous night. It also let the girl off the hook as far as pocketing any cash Astrapton had brought with him was concerned. The person who'd taken that, Satrius or whoever, must've been the guy's killer. 'She didn't say what the trouble was? Or where she was going?'

'No. I swear. I didn't know nothing about her boyfriend until the next day, when one of the other girls who works here went round to visit and found the body.'

'What about the neighbours? That late in the evening they'd be at home, right? No one saw or heard anything?'

He looked at me as if I'd grown an extra head. 'This is the Subura,' he said. 'Here you keep your doors locked after dark. You don't look outside them. And if you do hear anything that sounds like trouble you forget about it as soon as you hear it, because trouble is catching.

Besides, the flat opposite's empty.'

'Right. Thanks for your help, pal. You've been very informative.' I turned to go. 'By the way, you happen to know someone called Satrius?'

'Eutacticus's man?' He looked, suddenly, nervous. 'Yeah. Not personally, just the name.'

'You ever see him around here? Has anyone?'

'He the one who did it?'

Well, disreputable blot on the landscape the guy might be, but he was quick enough on the uptake. 'Just answer the question, pal.'

'No. No, I'm sorry. Can't help you there.'

I tried the magic word again. 'Not even if it's Eutacticus doing the asking?'

He was sweating, but he looked me straight in the eye. 'I've never even seen the man,' he said. 'That's the gods' honest truth. I swear it.'

Yeah, maybe. Still, I'd seen the effect Laughing George had on people like this poor bastard. Scylla and Charybdis came to mind: getting on the wrong side of either of them from choice was a bad, bad idea. And until the boss of Cupid's Bow personally saw Satrius's ashes shovelled into an urn I'd bet he wouldn't dare peach on him. Even then he'd probably think twice.

I left the guy to his beans.

SEVENTEEN

Right. The Pincian. Only I wouldn't hurry, to give Cleia a bit of breathing space and some time to talk things over with her brother. Not that I'd any fears that this would turn out a bum lead: the circumstantial side of her story had checked out at every turn, it fitted in with all the other facts and with the theory as well. Besides, the girl had been genuinely terrified at the thought of coming to see me at all.

So I killed a few hours in a friendly wineshop I knew on the way that had some decent wines on the board and rolled up at Eutacticus's gate when the sun was well into its third quarter.

'Go straight on in,' the guy on the gate said. 'The master's expecting you.'

'He is?'

'Yeah. Has been for the last couple of hours, at least.'

Shit; I didn't like the sound of this.

Eutacticus was in his study, talking to – or at, rather – a couple of guys I didn't know but who looked like heavies. He looked up with a face like thunder.

'What kept you, Corvinus?' he snarled.

'Uh...'

'Never mind, you're here now. You get the message?'

'What message?'

He sent the heavies out with a flick of a finger. They trooped past me with set faces. 'There've been developments. One of my clerks's been found dead with a knife wound in his belly and Satrius is missing.'

Oh, gods. 'Alexander?'

He stared. 'How the fuck did you know that? Sit down. We have to talk.'

I did. 'Okay. So tell me. What happened?'

'Not much to tell. One of the garden slaves found the body earlier this morning stashed behind a tree at the back of the house. I sent for Satrius to get him to fetch you but Critias couldn't trace him. The gate slave said he'd left the premises. What the fuck is going on here? And how the hell did you know about Alexander?'

I felt sick. 'Your daughter's maid came to see me this morning,' I said. 'She's Alexander's sister. She said that he'd told Satrius where to find Astrapton, the day before we went to the Subura and discovered the body.'

'The day *before?* But Satrius told me –'

'Right. Only he'd already killed the guy himself, the previous evening. I've just checked and it all works out.'

'*Satrius* killed Astrapton?'

'Yeah. Your stepson as well. At least, that's what it looks

like.'

'Gods!' Eutacticus sat back in his chair. 'That doesn't make sense.'

'Sure it does. Satrius was working for Paetinius. My guess is that he and Astrapton did the job together, on Paetinius's orders.'

'Satrius has been with me for years! I trusted the bastard!'

I shrugged. 'That's the theory. And it fits the facts, right down the line.'

'You're sure about this? One hundred percent, cast iron sure?'

'Yeah.'

He got up, made for the door, opened it and bellowed: '*Critias!*'

The major-domo must've been waiting in the corridor, because he was straight in.

'Yes, sir.'

'Put the word out. I want Satrius found. Tear the fucking city apart if you have to, but find him!'

The guy looked scared. 'Yes, sir.' He left.

'He'll've gone to Paetinius,' I said. 'Or at least that's my best bet. Where else could he go?'

'I'll get him.' Eutacticus came back to the desk and sat

down. 'Sooner or later. Don't you worry about that. And when I do the bastard won't die easy. As for Paetinius, I told you before, he's dead meat.'

Well, I'd reckon the jury was still out on that one. When I'd talked to him, Paetinius Senior hadn't seemed to be too concerned on that score, and Lippillus had said the guy had pretty considerable clout of his own. He'd've had to be fairly sure of his ground before he risked an all-out war with Eutacticus to begin with; he might even have decided the odds would be on his side when the shit hit the shovel and engineered the confrontation deliberately. Still, that was none of my concern; they were both crooks, and the pair of them could go to hell in a handcart with my blessing. In any event, I certainly wasn't going to broach the subject with Eutacticus himself. I kept my mouth firmly shut.

'You've done well, Corvinus.' Eutacticus was giving me his crocodile smile. 'Oh, sure, I wish things'd turned out different. Titus is dead, so is Astrapton, and like I said, I trusted that bastard Satrius, he was my right arm. And it appears I've lost a lot of cash, one way or another. But none of that's your fault, you've lived up to expectations. You can leave things to me now. Call the case closed. Like I told you at the start, you'll find me grateful.'

Fair enough. If the guy was happy – or at least the next thing to it – then he wasn't going to get any argument from me. Still, I had my professional pride to think of. 'Hang on, pal,' I said. 'There's just one loose end to tie up. This business of Larus.'

He frowned. 'Yes?'

'My guess is that the Seagull's a ship, not a person. That's about as far as I've got at present, but I was planning to go down to Ostia, ask around at the harbour. There're three possibilities I'd like to check out.'

'Astrapton's dead. Wherever he sent it, and however he did it, the money he stole's gone. That part of the story doesn't matter now. I've never been one to cry over spilt milk, Corvinus.'

'Yeah, well, put it down to unsatisfied curiosity. But I'd be happier myself to finish things with a tick in all the boxes. And that last crate wasn't sent until a few days ago. It could still be waiting for collection.'

'Fair enough.' He stood up and held out a hand. 'Do what you like. My thanks, in any case. I'll be in touch.'

I wouldn't be holding my breath, that was for sure: if I never saw the dangerous bastard again this side of an urn I wouldn't be crying either. Still, I shook the outstretched hand.

I was heading towards the stairs when the door to my left opened.

'Corvinus?'

Bugger; it was Sempronia. Not that I'd've minded another cosy téte-à-téte, but the chances were that Cleia would be there as well, and I was feeling bad enough about her brother already without having those mousey eyes fixed on me throughout the interview.

Sempronia must've read the thought in my expression.

'It's all right,' she said. 'I've sent Cleia to her room. She's very upset. She and Alexander were very close, and of course coming on top of Lynchus –'

'Yeah. Right.'

'Come in.'

I followed her inside and we sat on the facing couches.

'I wanted to catch you before you left, just to tell you that you needn't feel guilty about Alexander's death,' she said. 'If anyone was responsible, I was; I sent her to you, and it must've happened just after she left. She told you Satrius had seen her?' I nodded. 'Right. If I hadn't forced her to go he'd probably be still alive.'

'Maybe so,' I said. 'Mind you, my guess is that the poor guy was a dead man walking from the start. Not that I'd've even hinted that to Cleia. Satrius couldn't've let him

175

live. It was too risky, because sooner or later, one way or another, the business of the time discrepancy would've got out, your father would get to hear of it, and his goose would be cooked.'

'Not necessarily. My father wouldn't've taken Alexander's word over Satrius's.'

'Maybe not, lady. But what reason would Alexander have to lie? He'd have nothing to gain and a hell of a lot to lose. Your father's no fool. He'd've known that.'

'Possibly.' She put her chin in her hands. 'But why not kill him before? Or arranged things so that the death looked accidental, or something? Why wait until Alexander had told Cleia, let alone until Cleia had told me?'

I shrugged. 'Pass. Although we don't know for sure that Satrius knew the secret was out. He may've thought, or just hoped, maybe, that Alexander hadn't spotted the discrepancy at all.'

'Mm. That's not very likely, is it? Alexander wasn't stupid, and the whole household knew that Astrapton's whereabouts were still supposed to be a mystery until the morning his body was found. Which was why he mentioned it to Cleia in the first place.'

'Yeah. True.'

'Still. I hope Father finds him. Satrius, I mean. And he

will, eventually. It won't bring Titus back, of course, but I'd like to see him dead. Very much so.' I winced at the cool, matter-of-fact tone; they'd got a lot in common, father and daughter. 'So what now, Corvinus?'

'Not a lot. Your father says the case is closed, and that suits me. There's something I want to check over in Ostia, but that's just curiosity, a loose end. What about you?'

It was her turn to shrug. 'Marriage, I suppose. To Statius Liber, in a few months' time. I told you about him. Not something I'm particularly looking forward to, but I don't have much choice.' She stood up and held out a hand. 'Goodbye, anyway, and thank you for everything.'

Yeah. Right. Not the best close to a case I'd ever had, but like the lady had said you can't choose how things will pan out. I shook, and left.

EIGHTEEN

Next morning, we went through to Ostia. We'd set off early, before first light, with me on the mare and Agron and Cass in the wagon they'd used for the outward trip, so after dropping my bag off in the empty upstairs flat there was enough of the day left to make a start on the business side of things. Agron had told me my best plan would be to check with the harbour-master whether the three possible Seagulls were in port. He'd have addresses, too. So that's what I did. I was in luck: with less than a month of the sailing season left, they'd all finished their round trips and were berthed for the winter. I made a note of where to find the several owners and went back to settle in properly. Not, from the looks of things, that I'd have a very long stay; barring complications, I should be able to clear the thing up and be back home within a couple of days, easy.

I was up and out bright and early the next morning. Ostia isn't a big place, compared with Rome, and like any other town families involved in the same line of business tend to gravitate to the same area; so all three addresses were pretty close, near the harbour itself. I'd no reason to think one name was more or less likely than another, so I planned on taking them in the order Agron had given me:

Secundus, Imber and Florus.

I caught Secundus at breakfast; like Agron, in the bosom of his extremely large and boisterous family. In between the screams and general wrangling, I established that he'd never had a commission from anyone matching Astrapton's name or description. Scratch Seagull Number One.

Imber was out; his wife said I'd find him in one of the dockside wineshops getting an early skinful with his cronies. She didn't seem too happy about this, or particularly sympathetic towards anyone who had business with him, Roman purple-striper or not, so I thanked her politely, got the name of the wineshop and its precise location, and then pissed off to try Gaius Florus.

Florus's place – a tight little cottage at the end of an alleyway – was blissfully quiet. Which it might not have been, given that elderly widowers (which he was, Agron had told me the evening before) often live with their married daughters and, inevitably, assorted pack of grandchildren. On the other hand, he was almost stone deaf, which meant the interview on my side had to be conducted in short sentences with the words spaced out and shouted, with lots of repetition. All Florus's customers were local, and he'd dealt with the same ones for years. Scratch the Genua possibility.

Which left Imber. I was getting a bad feeling about this. Well, at least I'd be talking to him in a wineshop. And after fifteen minutes' strained conversation with Florus my throat was dry as a razor-strop.

I found the place. Not exactly your drinking-hole of choice, but I wasn't going to be picky. There were four or five nautical types at the bar, perched on stools and obviously settled in for the duration; I got the usual long stranger-in-the-room stare and a couple of nods before they turned back round and got on with the serious business of sinking the booze.

'What can I get you, sir?' the barman asked me.

I glanced at the board. None of the names were familiar: this being Ostia, I'd guess they were Spanish or Gallic imports. 'What would you recommend, pal?'

'The Lauronensian's good.'

'Okay. Make it half a jug.' I hitched myself up on a stool and turned to the local punters. 'Any of you gentlemen Gaius Imber?'

'That's me.' The guy next to me turned sideways.

'Valerius Corvinus. I'm making enquiries about a possible customer of yours. Guy called Astrapton. Ring any bells?'

'Nah. Not one of mine.'

'Greek. Early to mid twenties, good looking, snappy dresser. He'd be a regular. Four large crates over the past eight months, at about two month intervals between each crate. One of them held marble statues.'

He shook his head. 'Not me. The only regular orders I've had over the past year've been from local firms. And they've all been going on much longer than that.'

Bugger! 'You're sure? I was told the Seagull.'

'That's my boat right enough. Going west?'

'That I'm not sure about.'

'In that case you could try one of the other boats with the same name. Florus, he ships up the coast. Or there's Titus Secundus. He's on the Sicilian run.'

'I've tried them. They're not the ones either.'

'Then I'm sorry, pal. I can't help you.' He turned back to his wine and his mates.

Hell! Well, you couldn't win them all, and like Eutacticus had said finding the Seagull, man or boat, wasn't important any more. I'd've liked to've ticked the last box, though.

'Here you are, sir.' The barman put the half jug and a cup in front of me. I paid, filled the cup and sipped.

Not bad. Lauronensian, eh? That'd be Spanish. I'd have

to keep an eye out in future for that one.

Imber turned back round. 'Hang on, friend' he said. 'I've just had another thought. You sure the Seagull you want's an Ostian boat?'

'Uh-uh. That just seemed a reasonable bet. All I have to go on is the name.'

'Only there's Quintus Fulvius's. That's out of Massilia. He works the route from the other side.'

I felt the first prickle of excitement. 'You know where he'd happen to be at present?'

'Sure. Berthed at Quay Five. He's just got in. He'll be unloading and then taking on cargo for the return leg.'

'Quay Five. Great!' I downed the wine in a oner and passed him the rest of the jug. 'Here, pal, have this on me. Where's Quay Five?'

'Straight down to the harbour, turn left and it's about half way along. You can't miss it.'

'Got you! Thanks a lot!'

I left at a run.

*　　*　　*

Ostia may be in decline as a port, but it doesn't show where its harbour's concerned: if you don't know where you're going, even if like me you've got a good sense of direction, then the various quays, moles, sub-harbours and dead ends can be worse to negotiate than Minos's labyrinth. Also, when anyone uses the phrase 'you can't miss it' you can be cast-iron sure the place you're looking for'll be the devil to find. Finally, I was stopping every likely-looking punter I met and asking them for help, but it still took me a good half hour.

There were boats of different sizes moored nose to tail all along the stretch, but only one – the one at the far end – seemed to have any sort of activity connected with it. Yeah, Imber had said the captain – Fulvius, wasn't it? – would be unloading his incoming cargo. I made my way towards it between the various crates, bollards and general quayside lumber that filled a lot of the space between the storage sheds and the quay itself...

Which was when the guy jumped me.

He came out of the shed I'd just passed. I turned when I heard the footsteps, which was lucky, because the knife he was holding missed my back and sliced along the front of my tunic. I grabbed his arm and kneed him hard in the balls, then swung him round hard towards the quay's edge and let go.

He went over, into one of the boats: a good eight feet down. In the process, I heard the crack as the back of his head hit the edge of the stonework.

Shit. I looked where he'd fallen.

He was lying still, crouched up like a foetus, face hidden; his head at an angle, resting in a spreading pool of blood. There was an iron ladder let into the wall near the stern of the boat. I climbed down it and went to look, pulling the head back on the broken neck.

Publius Paetinius.

'Hey! What's going on?'

I looked up. A guy was standing on the quayside above me.

'You tell me,' I said. 'He came out of nowhere and tried to stick a knife in my back.'

'He dead?'

'Very much so.'

'Holy Neptune!'

'Yeah. Right.' I went back to the ladder and climbed up it. The guy was still staring down at Paetinius's corpse. 'I'll report it to the harbour-master, of course. You be a witness?'

'Sure.' He was looking sick. 'I'll be sailing first thing tomorrow morning, mind. If the wind's right.'

'Your name Fulvius?'

He gave me a sharp look. 'Yes. Yes, it is.'

'I was just coming to talk to you. Valerius Corvinus. You

carry some goods ever for a guy by the name of
Astrapton?'

'No. Not me.'

I repeated the description I'd given to Imber and the other
two. 'Greek, aged around twenty-five. Good looker, well-
dressed. The goods would've been packed in crates, four
of them, maybe more, shipped separately over the last
eight months.'

'You mean Quintus Philotimus. At least that's the name
he gave.'

Choirs of heavenly voices sang. 'It'll do, pal. Where were
they bound for ultimately? You have a delivery address,
or a name, maybe?'

He frowned . 'Hold on. What's this about? You're saying
the goods were stolen?'

'Yeah. Yeah, that more or less sums it up. I'm
representing the legal owner.'

'Massilia. For collection by a Titus Sestius. Which is
what's been happening. Up to now, anyway.'

Bull's-eye! I hadn't known where the now-defunct
Paetinius Junior's mother Sestia originated from, but I'd
bet now that it'd been Massilia. And that this Titus was a
brother, or at least a member of the same family. 'That
fits,' I said. I wasn't going to let on who the corpse below

us had been, mind, not even to the harbour-master: complications at this stage and this far from Rome and Lippillus I could do without. As far as the local authorities were concerned, at present at least, the guy had just been a common-or-garden mugger after my purse.

'So you'll want to lay your hands on Philotimus yourself,' Fulvius said.

'Uh…yeah.' I was guarded. 'That'd be a definite plus.'

'Then you're in luck. You'll be in Ostia for the next couple of days?'

'Sure. Longer, if need be. Why so?'

'Because he left the last of your four crates in storage. I've just put it on board. And he's sailing to Massilia with us himself. He arranged passage for two the last time I saw him, two months ago.'

'Passage for *two*?' Jupiter! I'd nailed Satrius!

'That's right. They may be here already, in fact. Staying in the lodging-house on the edge of town. That's where I was to send a message to, when the boat was ready to leave.'

'You happen to know who the other passenger is? Just for information.'

He told me.

NINETEEN

The lodging-house Fulvius had mentioned was on the coast, clear of the harbour complex itself but still inside the town boundaries. You don't see many places like that, but you do get them in the big ports: we'd stayed in one ourselves, in Brindisi, only a few months before when we'd gone to Alexandria. A variant on the country inn, but a lot more upmarket, catering for the travelling middle class who don't happen to have friends or relatives nearby but'd rather not be eaten alive before they sail by fleas and bedbugs. They can be pretty swish, the better ones, with self-contained apartments and catering laid on.

This place wasn't quite up to Brindisian standards, but it was pretty good all the same.

I went up to the guy on the reception desk.

'Yes, sir,' he said. 'Can I help you?'

'Yeah,' I said. 'I'm looking for a friend of mine, travelling to Massilia in the next few days.' I gave him the details. 'The boat's the Seagull, if it's any help. The captain was to send the message about sailing times here.'

'No problem, sir.' He smiled. 'They checked in a few hours ago.' Yeah, well, it would be 'they', still; young Paetinius would've been going too, if he hadn't presently been stiffening in an outhouse next to the harbour-master's office. 'Suite three, on the first floor.'

I went up, found the right door and knocked.

Cleia opened it. She looked at me, and her jaw dropped.

I put my finger to my lips.

'Who is it?' Sempronia said, from inside. Then, when I pushed past the girl, she saw me.

She was lying on one of the room's two couches with a bowl of grapes on the table in front of her. She put down the one she'd been holding and just stared.

I closed the door.

'Cleia, go into the bedroom.' Sempronia's eyes hadn't left my face. 'Stay there, please.' The maid meekly did as she was told, shutting the door behind her. 'Where's Publius, Corvinus?

'Dead.'

She just nodded. Her expression didn't change. I felt the first stirrings of anger: oh, sure, the guy had tried to kill me, but the poor bastard deserved more recognition than that. Not that her reaction was unexpected. I doubted if this bitch had ever given anyone else a second thought in her life. She was Eutacticus's daughter, all right, in spades.

'How did you know?' she said. Her voice was as empty of

emotion as her expression, and she might've been
asking me what the weather was like.

'I didn't. Or not before the captain of the Seagull told me
Philotimus would be travelling with his wife. It wasn't too
difficult to put two and two together after that.'

'No, I suppose not. Sit down. Would you like a grape?'

I didn't move. 'You and Astrapton killed Titus, right?'

'Oh, yes.' She took a grape from the bowl herself and
chewed it. 'It was quite easy. He was besotted with me.'

'Why?'

'Why did he have to die, you mean?' She shrugged. 'His
slave Lynchus had found out that Astrapton was
embezzling money from my father. How, I don't know, but
Lynchus always was a sneak, prying into things that were
no concern of his, and clever for a slave. Lynchus passed
the information on to Titus, and he brought it straight to
me. After the argument, he was planning to run off and
join his uncle anyway, and he arranged to meet me in the
grotto for one last time before he left. That part of it was
simple. He didn't suspect a thing.'

'You and Astrapton were lovers?'

She smiled. 'I wouldn't quite put it quite as strongly as
that. I let him think so, and he was amusing. Call him an
amusement, if you like. Like Titus was. Anyway, our

interests coincided. He needed a bolt-hole to escape to, I wanted to get away, with enough money to be independent for the rest of my life.'

'Convenient.'

For the first time, there was a flash of emotion in her eyes. 'Don't judge me, Corvinus! I've always loathed my father; he's a loathsome man. And marriage to Statius Liber, stuck down in Beneventum and used as a way of producing children, would've been a living death. Joining with Astrapton was the perfect business arrangement. And Paetinius and Mother jumped at it. As a way of getting their revenge on my father, it was ideal.'

'He'd've traced you eventually. Eutacticus.'

She shrugged. 'Massilia's a long way away, outwith even Father's reach. Mother's family, the Sestii, are big over there. And we chose the last trip of the season, before the sea-lanes closed for the winter, so we'd have plenty of time to prepare. I'd've been safe enough.'

'Married to Astrapton?'

'No. I told you, he was only an amusement. I would have worked something out.'

'Another convenient death?'

'Probably. It didn't come to that, though, did it? Or rather, it did. Just a bit earlier than I'd expected, that's all.'

Jupiter! She was a cold bitch, right enough! 'What about Satrius? You set him up, right?'

'Of course. That was your doing, Corvinus. As was most of it. If you hadn't stuck your nose in my father wouldn't've known about the embezzlement side of things until we were safely away, and Astrapton wouldn't've had to disappear earlier than planned. As it was, he fitted in quite well, and it gave me the breathing-space I needed.' She took another grape. 'The business with the Suburan girlfriend was absolutely genuine, by the way; I'd known all about it from the start, and I didn't mind, because if anyone had somehow been curious about his current entanglements it would've thrown them off the scent. The only lie involved Alexander. Yes, he told Satrius where to find him, but he did it the same morning Satrius told my father, not the day before, and by that time Publius had already been round to the flat and killed him.'

'So Alexander had to die too.'

'Mm.' She ate the grape. 'That was easy to manage. I did it myself, in fact. Once the body was found, I simply engineered a private word with Satrius and told him that I knew, through Cleia, that he'd had the information where to find Astrapton for almost a day before he'd passed it

191

on, and that I intended telling my father. Satrius wasn't a complete fool. He may have suspected something, but he knew his word alone wouldn't weigh over mine, and in any case he couldn't take the risk. So he ran.'

'Taking the heat off so that you could slip quietly down to Ostia.'

'Yes. Breathing-space, as I said. I only needed another couple of days, after all. I sent Cleia to you with strict instructions what to say, knowing that you'd think the case was over. Or at least, thinking it for the time it would've taken Father to trace Satrius, by which time the truth wouldn't matter because I'd be safely away. Only then you turned up and mentioned that you were going down to Ostia yourself. I knew you knew the name 'Seagull'– Astrapton was a fool to put that in writing, even though it might've seemed safe enough at the time – and the risk that you'd made the connection was too great to ignore, especially since time was running out.'

'So you contacted young Paetinius and cut and ran. You'd stay here while Paetinius kept an eye on the boat in case I turned up. Right?' I didn't wait for an answer. 'Incidentally, what sort of string did you keep him on, lady? I wouldn't've thought just a brother and sister relationship would be enough to persuade him to murder.

Either of Astrapton or me.'

'Oh, Paetinius didn't take much persuading,' she said. 'He was really quite a vicious little brute, and not all that clever. Also, he was very open-minded, sexually. The fact that it was incest, whether we had both a mother and a father in common or not, was a plus rather than otherwise, and it didn't worry me.' She smiled. 'Don't look so shocked, Corvinus! The old Egyptian kings did it all the time. Officially, of course, we were brother and sister – that held true as far as his father and Mother were concerned, and would have done on the trip over and beyond – but our private relationship was our own business. And, as you say, it did provide the necessary bond.'

I felt sick. 'And he'd meet with an accident as well, when you got to Massilia, yes?'

'Perhaps. If he'd proved difficult. Although being family he was more of a problem. Besides, it would probably not've been necessary by then. Ocean voyages this late in the season can be quite dangerous, and if we'd hit a patch of bad weather there was always the possibility that he might disappear overboard.' She smiled again. 'As you can see, I'm being quite candid with you about all of this.'

'Yeah,' I said. 'I'd been wondering about that. You

weren't hoping to get rid of me, too, after all, were you? Because –'

'Oh, no. Or at least not in the way you're thinking. I know that would be impossible.' She spread her hands. 'I'm not armed, and besides there could be no element of surprise, so I wouldn't stand a chance. No. I was going to make you a business proposition.'

'Namely?'

'The crate we were taking with us. Astrapton's last. It contains, I would guess, something just short of half a million sesterces in gold. Under the circumstances, I'm willing to lose that; I have enough in Massilia already to set me up very comfortably until I can make other arrangements. I'm suggesting a simple exchange. I have the captain unload the crate, you let me sail without it.'

'That wouldn't sit too well with Eutacticus, lady.'

'He'd never know. As far as my father's concerned, the money's gone already.'

'Plus I told the captain it contained stolen goods. He's an honest man, as far as I can tell. He's probably put it ashore with the harbour-master by now in any case.'

'Then you tell him you made a mistake. Or I have a word with him myself, see if he really is honest. I told you, over in Massilia I'm a rich woman, and the Sestii are a powerful family. The captain's a Massilian. One way or another, he'll be sensible about things.'

'And if I tell you to go to hell?'

She frowned; I honestly don't think she thought that she'd considered that possibility. Which told me a lot about sweet Sempronia. Mind you, as bribes went it was a pretty hefty one. 'That would be very stupid of you, in more ways than one. Believe me. After all, why should you care if I got away with things? My father forced you to become involved in this, you don't owe him anything, quite the reverse. If you come out of it half a million to the good, what does it matter?'

Gods! The chilling thing was that I could see she genuinely thought that it didn't.'

'People have died,' I said gently.

'A crooked accountant. A vicious thug. And a couple of slaves.'

'Plus your stepbrother.'

'Titus was nothing to you. You never even met him. What's the life of an actor's brat set against five hundred thousand sesterces?'

'It's enough. Go to hell.'

She flinched, as though I'd slapped her. 'My father will never take your word against mine,' she snapped. 'And when I persuade him – as I will – that this is all a mistake I'll see you buried!'

'I'll take that chance, lady,' I said. 'Now go and get your cloak. We're going down to the local Watch office where they can make arrangements for you until I can get word to your father where you are.'

She got up without a word and went into the bedroom.

I waited for a good five minutes before the door opened again. But it wasn't Sempronia. It was Cleia, and she was holding a knife at arm's length, like it was a snake. The front of her tunic was a mass of blood.

She dropped the knife and just stood there, head lowered.

Oh, shit! I pushed past her through the open door…

Sempronia was lying slumped over the dressing table. That was covered with blood too, which, considering her throat had been cut, wasn't surprising. I came back out. Cleia hadn't moved.

'Uh…you care to tell me what happened?' I said gently.

'I killed her, sir.' The usual mouse's whisper. She didn't look up. 'While I was tidying her hair.'

'Where did you get the knife?'

'From the travelling trunk. It was open beside the bed.'

'You, uh, want to explain why?'

'She was evil. She murdered Lynchus and Alexander.'

'Yeah. I know. But –' How could I put this? Slaves are brought up from birth to see themselves as goods, not people. Oh, sure, they have feelings and emotions like anyone else, but they're conditioned to keep them buried where necessary, whatever the provocation. For a slave to murder her master or mistress just isn't done, the worst crime possible; not just from a legal viewpoint but more important in the mind of the slave herself. The fact that it's a fast shortcut to an inevitable and very painful death helps reinforce things too: there are no extenuating circumstances, none, not under any conditions; our society can't afford to let there be. Cleia would die, that was sure; quickly, if she was lucky, but almost certainly not. Much more likely was slow and systematic torture, followed by crucifixion.

'She was getting away with it,' she said. 'Oh, she'd have got round the master, like she told you. I was listening, I heard every word, and she was right: he'd take her word over anyone's, believe anything she told him. It was the only way to make sure she got what she deserved. I was going to do it anyway, on the ship, if I got the chance, and then throw myself overboard. Don't worry, sir, I won't give you no trouble.'

I hesitated. Then I decided. It'd be easier that way, for all concerned.

I picked up the knife, went into the bedroom, put it on the dressing table beside Sempronia's outstretched hand, and came back out.

'Okay, Cleia,' I said. 'Let's go.'

TWENTY

I rode the mare back to Rome next morning, after squaring things with the Ostian authorities and telling them where to send the news; I'd left Cleia with Cass and Agron for collection, stressing to her how important it was to remember that Sempronia had committed suicide when she'd seen the game was up. I still had to have a long talk with Eutacticus, of course, and that I wasn't looking forward to; but I reckoned I'd done enough trotting back and forth to the Pincian at his behest for a while. Besides, I wanted to wait until the dust settled. Another day wouldn't matter.

Bathyllus was looking smug when he opened the door for me.

'Welcome back, sir,' he said. 'Did you have a pleasant trip?'

'Uh...yeah. Yeah, it was all right.' I took the cup of wine he held out. 'The mistress around?'

'Yes, sir. Oh, and we had a bit of excitement ourselves while you were away.'

'Really? What was that?'

'The mistress will explain. She's in the atrium.'

I went through, bemused. Perilla was lying on the couch, reading. I gave her the welcome-home kiss and lay down opposite.

'Well, dear?' she said.

'Case solved,' I said. 'I'll tell you about it in a minute. What's this bit of excitement Bathyllus mentioned?'

'Ah.' She hesitated. '"Excitement" isn't exactly the word. It was more of an accident, really.'

'What?'

'It happened while I was out.'

'Come on, lady! Meton drop the soup pot? Get his fingers caught in the mincer? Bathyllus was looking smug as hell, so it must've been something along those lines.'

'Daistratus fell off a step-ladder.'

'*What?*'

'And broke his arm.' She glared at me. 'Marcus, it is *not* funny! The poor man was in terrible pain, Bathyllus said.'

I tried to straighten my face. 'Tell me more.'

'He was working on the top part of the mural in the dining-room. The cord holding the two parts of the step-ladder must've been frayed, and the thing collapsed. He fell on his arm – his right arm – and broke it.'

'His, uh, right arm. The one he uses to paint with.'

'Yes. Bathyllus sent for Sarpedon, of course' – Sarpedon was our doctor – 'and he set the bone and put the arm in splints. But he said it'd take several months to heal properly.'

'This, uh, means that Architecturescape Seven's on hold, then, does it?'

'Unfortunately, yes. Or rather, it's been cancelled altogether.'

'Really?'

'I arrived home just as Daistratus was leaving. I was able to have a quick word with him.' She ducked her head. 'I'm afraid he was rather emotional.'

'Was that a smile, lady?'

She ignored me. 'He didn't intend to sue, he said. However, in view of the circumstances and his earlier conversation with you he flatly refused to complete the work at a future date. The phrases "artistic philistine" and "pearls before swine" were used. The upshot was that we agreed on a refund of half what I'd originally paid him.'

'Reasonable.'

She sniffed. 'I thought so. Particularly since the poor man will be incapacitated for some time to come.'

'The world of art can only be grateful for the respite.'

Bathyllus soft-shoed in carrying the rest of the jug.

'Will there be anything else, sir?' he said. 'Dinner will be quite late this evening, Meton says, but I can ask him to make you an omelette if you're hungry after your ride.'

'No, that's okay,' I said, holding up the winecup for a refill. 'Oh, Bathyllus, just out of interest. That step-ladder. The one Daistratus fell off.'

'Yes, sir?'

'It collapsed because the cord was frayed, right?'

'Indeed. Very unfortunate.'

'Yeah. A bit sloppy on your part, wasn't it? I mean, making sure everything in the household's shipshape, tight as a drum, safe as houses and running along smoothly is a major-domo's job.'

'Yes, sir. I wouldn't have expressed it in quite that mixture of metaphors myself, but I have to agree. An inexcusable dereliction of duty, sir. I feel extremely guilty.'

'Well, we'll let things ride this time, little guy. No use crying over spilt milk. Water under the bridge.'

'Quite, sir. Thank you.'

He turned to go.

'Oh, Bathyllus?'

'Yes, sir?'

'You wouldn't happen to have a bucket of lime-wash handy, would you?'

'I think that could be arranged, sir.'

'For use before dinner?'

'I'll see to it at once.' He exited.

Ah, well. We'd just have to eat looking at a blank wall for a while longer.

Maybe, if Eutacticus was really grateful, I could screw the price of a new mural out of him.

———————————————

CPSIA information can be obtained at www.ICGtesting.com
Printed in the USA
LVOW071003181012

303413LV00004B/27/P